Cordelia's
Compendium of Characters

By Cordelia Malthere

Edition 1

Published by Malthere Publications Limited

Find out more about the author and her books at
http://www.cordelia-malthere.co.uk

If you want to become a published author visit
http://www.malthere-publications.com

ISBN:978-0-9931450-4-9

Graphics by White Tiger Designs

This book is dedicated
To all my fans and readers.
Enjoy the ride into
My Universes,
As much as
I enjoy
Creating
My Worlds of Words.

In particular,
It is dedicated,
To one of my first readers,
A wonderful individual and colleague,
Sandra Dean.
Bless your cotton socks
For having
Followed
All my baby steps,
As an Author.
XXX

Cordelia Malthere

Preface

The intention behind the creation of the Compendium of Characters is to give a ready guide to anyone who ventures into the Maltherian Universes. It is a vast place where my books act as planets with their own particular orbits and trajectories, inhabited by colourful characters intricately interacting with each others. The Compendium maps the revealed territories of the published stories. It reveals with parsimony some unchartered ones as well, making one envisage the beyond and the further. This guide will be expanded each time more of my novels are released in to the public domain to provide the ultimate companion to my printed work at any point in time.

Exploration of the micro-cosmos of each story in its own right, the Compendium offers the 'who's who' of my Characters. As an Author, I live everyday in a fantasy world where my characters, heroes, heroines and baddies form my fantastic family where I know all its members intimately down to a 't'. Somehow sometimes I feel that they are my everything from best friends to life long partners. They knock on the doors of my imagination, individually, one day, unannounced and stay with me forever. They help me transcend, understand better and deal with my daily life. Not unlike a child's imaginary friends, or James Stewart's 'Harvey', that giant invisible rabbit that follows him everywhere, my characters, down to their pets, like 'Geddy' the Dra-Rex, the half dragon half tyrannosaurus with a canary brain, who eats demons for breakfast, occupy me day and night. If you see me sitting on the train, commuting quietly, not noticing the other passengers, time or stations that go by, I am probably lost on a chair, a director's one, visualising a scene, and asking to its actors to do it one more time, with more passion, just for the pleasure of it. At night, my keyboard will receive all the results of the seemingly absent moments of my day when I dived into my creative fantasy worlds. Sometimes it will collect the fruits of another gathering altogether, when I paid attention, observed, maybe a particular individual of interest whose encounter results in a caricature of words of some sort or a moment where acts will be transcribed, woven into my work, exaggerated or not.

Writing is for me, more than I can say. I would describe the feeling like the one that a tame little white goat, with a singing bell at her neck, which has been enclosed in a dark stable full of stinking rotted straw all Winter, experiences on her release to the gloriously green and lush mountain pastures for the Summer. More than pure escapism, writing makes me analyse the stable in its every single corner and detail in order to make sense of it, whistle blowing it, accept it or reject it, totally or in part. I find writing not only pleasurable but therapeutic. It made me be who I am now. It helped me grow from all my experiences.

To explain this by an autobiographic example, the day I planned to throw myself under a train with a depressed exactitude, down to the minute, I stood there, in front of a passing train, alive and well, still, with a retaining scream in my head. It was a commanding 'Hold on you do not know what's up there or if there is an up there. Make her fall under the track. Stay on them, write it.' On the Barnet tracks, the trains left, there was a dead pigeon, grey yet colourful, red and green feathers on its chest, wings spread open, laying lifeless. I didn't know how long the bird had been there, but I took my normal train on the opposite platform flying back to what my nest was in that troubled time. That night, I wrote about what was up there and 'Clementine Boatswain', who took the big plunge for me, was born. She endorsed my shortcomings and struggles. Her adventures in the After-World were blogged regularly. Her story will be re-published. Writing her took me out of depression right and proper. She led me onto a different track altogether.

Her success was consequential enough to make me believe upon my abilities, build upon them, and start creating my own path. Director of my own publishing company and author, my Characters took me on a memorable journey, a trip of a lifetime, and I hope they will do the same to you all.

Let me take the honour of presenting them to you, for they are my dearest friends,

Let me lead you forward to their fantastic worlds that mirror ours,

Let's take the plunge onto the unchartered track together,

Xxx

Cordelia Malthere.

The Compendium of Characters.

This comprehensive nomenclature will be ordered by the chronology of the published books and within it sometimes by the alphabetical order of the characters.

Following the 'Who's Who' of characters, you will find a 'What's what' section, a list of created or combined words with their meanings in a future Compendium. There are a fair few occasions where I applied this poetic license to fit closely to the heartbeat of the story or a particular individual within it. The last sections are the peep-holes to the future publications relating to those stories, spin-offs, prequels or next instalments to look forward to. It will offer the tangible glimpse of what is coming next or what happened before.

You will have to bear in mind that what I let out in the open in any given time is a small portion of the rest, of my inner fictional Universes which have been created since I could draw creatures from foxes to unicorns, hence decades. Others fancy building houses during that time which they can not take to their graves, yet I have learnt that my body is my only property to take elsewhere, my words and actions to be, are my only legacy.

Drawings and sometimes pictures are illustrating characters. I will offer the description of some characters as I see them but also they came about to be in my mind. The Who's who sections will benefit of numerous quotes to enrich the portraits of each character. Like living beings, they evolve instalment after instalment, adding to their complexity. The self secure Archangel Gabriel found in the first tome of It-666 differs from the shadow of himself he becomes in later tomes because in the fifth instalment, he does the unthinkable, something with deep consequences for everyone, even himself.

Put your seatbelt on and enjoy the ride. First destination is Wilton Town in the little hours past midnight, there is a racket going on in the cemetery...

Hair Rising, Heir Raising, Erasing.

Published the 21st of October 2014, this short story was born like many of my stories within the midst of a nightmare. I remember still vividly hearing some chilling noises, some eerie music, sad laughter, stuck in the darkness of a long box. I pushed the door open to realise that I was in my coffin. A cowardly glance outside revealed a hilly cemetery, a moonlight night and other corpses rising from their graves, some dragging others to do so. I was freaked enough at the sight to lay back in the safe darkness, thinking that it must be a bad dream and that it will all pass. But someone saw me, someone recognised me, called my name out loud and opened my coffin lid wide open. In front of that half decomposed cadaver, my heart seemed to fail to beat any longer. I closed my eyes of fright and I woke up in my bed safe and well. I was not exposed in a coffin, exhibited to other dead people, I was in my bedroom with for only witness, my black cat Mystic blinking her yellow eyes at me peacefully from the other pillow.

That morning, still haunted by the dream, my mind went on overdrive with the what if I had followed that corpse calling my name who I recognised as someone that passed away. It felt like being 'Ebenezer Scrooge' visited by ghosts. Drawing on Charles Dickens 'A Christmas Carol', I set out to write 'Hair Rising, Heir Raising, Erasing'.

Abraham Wilton-Cough was born proudly that day in a coffin and on paper. I must admit that the day I wrote his last expiring lines, I cried. One can call him an anti-hero, easily. That character took my place in that cemetery and went into the journey I did not take myself. I often do that (Clementine Boatswain is another creation resulting of steps I did not do). Abraham had to live that unbearable sense of exposure I endured for a split second for the length of the story.

A. It disturbed me greatly. I would sing out loud I am free from faults and crimes and swear it on any ready holy book of any kind. Proudly, I would stand my ground then say I have done no wrong. You may not be a broad day light criminal, or a night one, a rapist, a thief or whatever big crime implies, hopefully not a brain washed terrorist, but whatever we say or swear, we all have the niggling mistakes that will keep you awake at night. We may ignore them or not even see them, depending on how pride cover your eyes. After that dream, I questioned myself deep down, why did I feel that bad? Being a good individual, I went to dig any dirts I may have made: Mum is ignoring me for seven years, I will do likewise after failing to reach her out many times. To the day, our relationship is still a thin thread ready to break up at anytime for long periods. Can we afford it? With only one life to live? What is the damages on her side and mine? I resolved that my unease was all about what I took for granted like a family. How we are dealing with one another is most important for all involved. I wanted Abraham Wilton-Cough to carry that essential message.

B. Although Abraham is passing away at the end of the story, he has been given that chance to realise what were his mistakes. It took the removal of his great pride where one feels comfortably always right and all others are obviously so wrong. It took a journey from grave to grave. It took a feverish nightmare at the end of his own life's journey. Able to rectify, do some erasing of his past mistakes for a few minutes, Wilton-Cough did so with a heart warming humbleness and the remaining of his heroic proud guts that were shot hours earlier protecting his customers.

The structure of the story is made of three parts flowing together forming the complete journey of Abraham Wilton-Cough which follows the rhythm of the title. First comes the 'Hair Rising' where the hero faces the fact that he is a rising dead in the town cemetery. Disturbingly as there are other walking dead, the realisation that it may be a judgement night, an apocalypse of some sort unsettles the character. His guide, Amelia Bates, is the individual that bothers his conscience, the widow which he made pregnant. She is the one that walks him from grave to grave to face the music, his heirs, and errors in the second part, the heart of the story, the 'Heir Raising'. Finally he meets his last conception, a child which defies all his preconceptions being an Angel. She gives back to the wondering and wandering spirit of Abraham the consciousness he needs to put some things to right prior to his imminent death. On his death bed, lay Wilton-Cough doing all the erasing he can, in the third and last past of the novel, 'the Erasing'.

Enough said, let's meet the characters...

Abigail Bates.

Illegitimate daughter of Abraham Wilton Cough and Amelia Bates, Abigail was not conceived out of love. She is a pure mistake, simply made by her respective parents out of drunkenness. Despite her controversial conception, even unborn she is a blessing to all.

To her guilt ridden father, the mere fact that she is the growingly visible result of his action within the belly of the Widow Bates caused his nagging unrest and prophetic nightmare on his death bed. Her unseen presence pushes the proud Abraham first to admit that he did commit mistakes during his lifetime. With her mother playing the spiritual guide to the departing soul of Abraham, they help him to go from admission to making amends, passing by the acknowledgement of his errors.

'Hair Rising, Heir Raising, Erasing' is a tragi-comedy of errors: Wilton Cough's ones with his heirs to be, his very own family. The play on words in the title is truly evocative of his entire nightmarish journey. It asks fundamental questions about how we raise our children. Are we partial to one and not the other? Are we imposing our views on them, destroying their talents in the making in brutal psychological ways? Did we simply show love to the ones we love when we had the chance of an entire lifetime to do so? Were we so head strongly proud and confident we were right that we hurt many in the making, in our path?

Home truths hurt. Abigail hurts the still living day life of Abraham. She is one he has yet to confess out loud to his lawfully wedded wife, minutes away from his death. However his wounded guts managed to find the strength to do so because the Angel that Abigail is, pushes is dying soul back to consciousness, giving him a short window to correct his errors, to do some sort of serious erasing.

Abigail's character works as the sum of errors of any put to right. From refusing to acknowledge her as his own child, Abraham, meeting her finally, is mesmerised by her Angelic Being. She embodies more than what his legitimate sons achieved to be in their own after-lives.

In his premonitory feverish dream prior to his death, Abraham is allowed to see a night where the dead are rising. It constitutes a terrifying journey for him where the fate of his illegitimate daughter provides him with a much needed breather.

Abigail's life is described to him by her proud mother Amelia within the Mausoleum that contains her daughter's remains. Suitably impressed and chastised, Wilton-Cough expresses the wish to have done better with his own life: his dying wish. He is granted it by being allowed to be conscious for his remaining minutes of expiring life.

If that Angelic character brings about the redemption of her own father prior to his death, she is also a blessing in many ways to her human mother, the lonely good sweetheart that is Amelia Bates. For Abigail provides her finally with the family, the widow had craved for the many years of her childless marriage. She is a providential heavenly gift who repairs Harry Bates' lack of progeniture to his loving wife on his funeral night.

Was Harry given a last death wish to his own soul and was the result little blessed Abigail given to Amelia? If you do not know, Amelia's life is turning completely around in consequences of the birth of her only child. From lonely, she becomes a mother to all the tiny mistakes of Wilton Town, to all its unwanted children given to her big heart to be cared for.

The humble home of Amelia Bates provides the love to numerous souls created by mistakes, and offers to them the tools for a better future. The exchange is love for love. The Widow Bates is loved and respected by all for eternity. Her grave bestows a eulogy and his constantly decorated by flowers.

Abigail when born ends up on Amelia's doorsteps where she pretends to find her upon the forever forgiving Father Odell's plan. From that point on, the Widow finds many babies on her doorsteps which her heart adopts without question.

The questionable existence of Abigail fades in the fact that she is. Angelic from the start or from her human's life cannot be argued either way. She is an Angel.

Scarce, yet forever in the background of Abraham's conscience, his daughter only says one sentence to him:

'Abigail, spreading her white wings majestically before her father took his bony hands within hers then whispered before pushing him into the deep hollow that was her own grave within the mausoleum,

-It is quarter to three. Your wish is granted, Soul, however you have only minutes to repair what you can.'

Abraham Wilton-Cough

We meet Abraham Wilton-Cough as a skeleton in the feverish nightmare he is having on his death bed. Our Anti-Hero rise from his coffin to reluctantly follow the Widow Bates on a journey to discover what happened to his heirs.

The self centred and self satisfied Wilton-Cough would have preferred to remain in the cosy safety of his coffin to carry on ignoring the World. However Amelia Bates pushes him literally outside of his comfort zone and boundaries to face the music during that autumnal night of the dead. Her convincing arguments challenges the pride of Wilton-Cough enough to have him follow her. But instead of being proved right, Abraham is shown how wrong he has been during his life.

The story truly starts with what is troubling his conscience: the mistake he did one night with the Widow Bates. His refusal to admit it and the consequences of it are tackled by a crafty Amelia who appeal onto his great pride. If Abraham knows by heart his illustrious ancestors, acknowledges his important position in their lineage, he would recognise a descendant of his, who raises his pride.

That strategy doesn't fail to bring the character following the footsteps of Mrs Bates to check out what became of his own two legitimate sons out of utter curiosity but also wanting to know more about his illegitimate daughter.

Abraham Wilton-Cough is a proud character yet he is not a proud father for multiple reasons which have more to do with himself rather than his children. One question haunting his dream is how he raised his boys. The answer and to his own admission was with partiality but also with some psychological pressure. His favoured eldest, Zachary was taught to become like him, strongly insensitive to become a prosperous man. Whilst his talented youngest son, Josiah, was strongly discouraged to follow his own heart, passion, and pursuit to follow the one of his father which was making money instead. The results of his fatherhood shown to Wilton-Cough in that staunch premonitory nightmare filled him with self-shame. The realisation that he lacked all his life the ability to comprehend his children hits him suddenly very hard like a slap across his face. It becomes a reciprocal emotional battering, from Josiah refusing to acknowledge him as a father to Zachary who sees his skeleton as potential food to feed upon, having become a materialistic dead: a zombie.

Last but not least as a man, Abraham is not proud to have fathered an illegitimate child for despite not being demonstrative, he dearly loves his wife Angela. To acknowledge his posthumous daughter is to acknowledge that he was far from perfect. In a nutshell, Abigail is the bombshell that makes him admit all his past mistakes and errors. She makes him lose his intrinsic pride to embrace for once in his life humble pie.

Wilton-Cough is far from being a proud husband, similarly it has nothing to do with his wife but all to do with him and own insecurities. This is where we meet the bitterness of the character. The physically unremarkable Abraham secured the attention of the beautiful Angela, an Italian shopkeeper's daughter: he had no doubts it was all because of what his name and money represented to her. Under that misconception came the excuse for the treatment of his wife, jealously kept indoors only to be submitted to a daily mental battering. The cherry on the cake comes with his last will which will leave his wife and the son she likes most, Josiah, destitute and at the mercy of his eldest, Zachary. The consequences of that bitter written will of his are presented to him during his journey from grave to grave. His visit to Angela's pauper's mass grave and the knowledge of her fate affects him deep down. This is where the character meets full sorrow, ignored by whom he loved most but who he had also treated constantly in an overbearing fashion during his life.

In this whimsical nightmare, Abraham Wilton-Cough is almost the caricature of his more serious, stern and sarcastic real self. Creating this character has been a roller coaster ride of emotions. Writing him made me laugh but also cry. When the hero is pushed back to the realm of consciousness, and wakes up in an ordinary yet cosy bedroom of the 19th century, the seriousness of his state is clear cut. We have a dying man on his bed who has been shot. Bad or not, Wilton-Cough, despite him not thinking of himself as heroic, was wounded protecting his customers in his bank. He refuses to be acknowledged as a hero in an honest sarcasm who revealed his true motivation behind his action: his customers are useful to his business alive not dead. It makes money sense to protect them. This highlights his true character, nature and what motivated his entire life to the point where Wilton-Cough is very aware of the irony of his fate.

However late it is in his life to rectify anything, he makes the desperate attempt to do so with his last minutes. I had tears writing the character's last lines and words in the part that constitute the 'Erasing' of the book title, the one where Abraham Wilton-Cough tries to erase what he can from the errors of his ways. This last part of the story is where the emotional journey of the main character ends after having him rewrite another last will which will create a better future for all the other characters, members of his family. That new future is scope for another story where Wilton-Cough maybe raised from the dead again as a ghost, haunting his loved ones to prevent them making mistakes... Dear Abraham until we meet again, I will forever cherish your memory as my first published main character.

This character has been inspired by Charles Dickens's 'Ebenezer Scrooge'. The main similitude is a proper wink, which is his profession as director of the first bank of Wilton Town, a banker. Finding a name that resonated right for the type of hero, Abraham Wilton-Cough was in my mind, posed no difficulty.
The morning of the dream, Abraham was created, almost like a corn will pop in a pan to make popcorn, like someone bursting to my psyche fully formed, with a delightful bite and crunch to him.

I put that character in the uncomfortable shoes I wore during my nightmare. I had to dress him with the feelings I had pushing the lid of a coffin, my coffin. Terrified and wondering about what was going on out there, yet cowardly willing to nestle back to the grave as the safest place on earth was one of them. Another one was the sentiment of being laid bare, exposed, yet not knowing what wrong did I do to feel that way, proudly I would have said, I have nothing to regret. Scratching my head to find any possible wrongs I could have done, the very morning I woke up, my answers came forward fast and clear, it had to do with family relations, your loved ones: things you do and don't, like not talking to someone for seven years, for whatever reasons which brought the initial clash, with the pride and stubbornness on both part kept alive until it subsided back to love. Am I proud of that fact under my belt? The answer is no. So my Abraham is very much a family man who did cock things up a bit with his loved ones in ways which can be seen as acceptable in broad day light, as none dared to challenge him, yet the damages done in the heart of his family is profound. His heirs are drifting apart in the cemetery, with only two maintaining a loving relationship with each other, few and far between.

His surname had to be double-barrelled to represent a sense of pride and patriarchal endorsement. He is part of the lineage which founded Wilton Town. I wore a double-barrelled name for nine months with some vanity. It made me feel more important than I was, especially that during that time I felt lower than I ever felt before. Abraham had to endorse the mistake that my double-barrelled name was, upon his heavy cloak. Let's peel the onion of his created name. First there is the Wilton. In my mind it carries many meanings regarding to 'Will' and 'Willpower'. It is 'Will-ton': The tune of one's will. When there is a will, there is a tune singing somewhere of hope, good or bad. 'Ton' means tune in French. Wilton-Cough's amount of will has the power to change the lives of his loved ones for the worse or the better. This first syllable of his surname also symbolise that formal piece of document, the one that carries your will to others beyond your grave, your last wishes. Some of us, organised and well prepared for any eventuality have those ready long before their last breath. The document represents your wishes at the point in time you formulated it. What happens if you moved on far from those wishes as you expire? Were they drawn in a bitter moment of your life where you cut out some totally, just to feel a little better? What if you are all reconciled and the forgotten will is unearthed and enforced like a battle axe destroying your own family at your death? What if you are dying with a ravaging bitterness, proudly unashamed? What is the tune of your own will?

Wilton-Cough represents all those questions which could be resumed to: Are your last wills for the better or the worse? Forgetting that, imposing your own will to others during your life, raise another question: the one of free will. The question of will runs through the story as the main theme and finishes with the character having the opportunity to change his at the last minute.

About 'ton' meaning tune: Abraham Wilton-Cough is facing the music on his death bed. From the cacophony he wakes up to in his grave, to the cuckoo clock striking 3 am, announcing he has only 13 minutes to live, passing by the forest clearance haunted by his son Josiah and his powerfully eerie tunes, the character is caught by the music. So much so that he choses his last tune for his body to depart, to be played by Josiah, 'La Marche Funébre' de Chopin, a funeral march created the very year of his death, 1837.

The Cough part in the surname is just a spitting out loud of everything that can make you choke: From the suppression of your own free-will by someone, family, peers, to cheer mistreatment if you do not follow their own wishes and wills. On Earth, sadly, some will accept your murder by overbearing criminals as the better option. For they do not know any better than a falsely created honour, pride which make them do crimes in broad day light or accept them as common currency. 'Father, forgive them, for they do not know what they are doing.' Luke 23:34.

Abraham has two sons which he raised with partiality. The eldest takes it all whilst the youngest fights to keep his mum and himself with some sort of living in the street of Wilton Town. Well those are the consequences foreseen in Wilton-Cough's dream caused by his first last will. Now the choice of Wilton-Cough's first name was inspired by the biblical patriarch. As Abraham was ready to sacrifice his god given son Isaac to god's will, Wilton-Cough was ready to sacrifice his eldest son's soul, Zachary by spoiling him by his own will. Abraham Wilton-Cough is visited on his death bed, in his feverish nightmare by his own daughter, the Angelic Abigail, who gives him back the few minutes of consciousness he needs to correct his will. Will that be enough to save the soul of Zachary?

After peeling the layers of Wilton-Cough, lets meet him in the core and in quotes:

'-Well, well, well, I'll be damned, we can't sleep in peace anymore. What is that cacophony all about?

A skeletal hand pushed open its coffin lid grumpily and a bewildered dishevelled skull appeared, peering outside full of suspicion.'

'Then Abraham added with deep sadness in his voice,

-Was I that despicable? I'd better do as he told me and wait to turn to dust.

Presenting her hand with a look full of kindness, Amelia Bates ordered,

-Come with me. Let's find out together.'

'Catching a last glimpse of his son, Abraham moved along the path, deeply sighing, and started to talk to himself to try to quench his incredible sadness,

-Yes, see you later. I thought you would appreciate to see me gutted somehow, my now little big fruit of my loins. Awesome ghost, you are, very... very scary. Look, I am somehow moving towards any of the directions you pointed to me tonight. Oh my, oh my, when I dreaded a slow dusting alone in my grave, now I am walking towards worse. What have I done? What have I done? Oh my, Oh my. It would be such a lovely evening to rise truly if I had not cocked up so beautifully my life. It is warm like an Indian summer. The moonlight is just, just mesmerising, glowing upon everything: the path, the graves and their robbers. Robbers, thieves, my grave, they are doing my grave among many... Oi!

Waving his arms erratically Wilton-Cough went running forward in an incentive to protect all graves and especially his own one. He tried the very fearsome and ghostly 'Ouuuuh, ouuuuh' and the more immediate 'schoouuuh, schouuuuh' but the effect was not what he expected.'

'Wilton-Cough watching his last will burn to ashes offered a sorrowful smile to his wife and children,

-Yes, I did say plenty of things along those lines, but the fact and the truth are as I am at my last minutes, that I must admit that I was entirely wrong many times, for I have no right to impose upon you to live your very own lives a certain way that suits me and no others. The three of you are free to live your lives as you desire, to follow your own dreams. Make the most of every minute for they do count and never forget that there is only one rule to be respected...

A painful burst of cough stopped his words as Abraham tried to catch his breath, with the desperate hope that it was not his last.'

Catch up Abraham Wilton-Cough's last moments while you can and let him whisper to you what he learnt from his journey beyond the grave.

Amelia Bates.

Her shrieking voice is the dreaded and familiar one which guides Abraham Wilton-Cough during the night of the rising dead. Born Elroy, the widow Bates has the privilege to be Abraham's impoverished neighbour. Always in the now and know, Amelia is his perfect guide.

Amelia Bates is a lively character: The woman next door, married to a soldier, alone and childless, who knows everything about anyone, aka your perfect nosy neighbour. She is the gossipping widow from whom all news of the neighbourhood and further are broad-casted, rather colourfully and bluntly than not. She reports things as she sees them with her own sensitivity and at her own doorsteps.

February 1801 saw Amelia breathe for the first time in the very crowded yet loving Elroy family. Her Irish father came to Wilton Town to settle. The Elroy's eleven strong brood of children were all an asset to the small town in their own right. They could have been twelve yet their mother passed away giving birth to her last child, a boy who did not survived very long afterwards.

From her tough early days, Amelia learnt love and what it meant to individuals within a family. This is also why she is the appointed guide to Abraham Wilton-Cough. She is able to pin-point and show him his wrong doings plainly like no other. At each blows/ home truths, her hand and voice help the hero move along and get back together. She is a provider of heart warming comfort, for being a big heart, she knows what love is and how to spell it.

Amelia was only sweet sixteen when she was married to Harry Bates. Although it was a marriage of love, it also provided a certain respectability and standing to her. She lived in a small modest flat in the well off part of the town. Her husband soldier however was hardly ever there. Going from war to missions Harry left behind his wife so frequently that the lone Amelia occupied herself with all the livings surrounding her. From learning to read just to be able to be in the know of what was going on around her and the world, to spreading the news and latest gossip, this ardent newspaper reader was filling up the sorrowful result of Harry's absences which was their inability to build their own family.

Her husband's death abroad happened during a prolonged military campaign which took him away from his wife for five long years. The devastated Mrs Bates, drowning her sorrow in alcohol the night of the funeral, is in such a state that her neighbour Wilton-Cough helps her back to her flat. But almost as drunk as her, his offered comforting shoulder turned rapidly into a sexual embrace.

Returning to his senses, Abraham Wilton Cough realises his mistake and adultery in his case, by brushing it under the thick carpet of silence. However the exert of one drunken night was enough for the widow Bates to fall pregnant. Despite all his will to ignore the fact and result of his mistake, the increasing waistline of his neighbour is a constant stark reminder of his guilt.

On his death bed, only a few months after the one of Harry Bates, a feverish Abraham is haunted by a vivid nightmare where Amelia Bates takes his hand to guide him to see the results and consequences of his deeds and actions.

The vision of the widow Bates in his dream plays like the agent of his conscience reminding him and showing him all that troubled him or not of his past actions which were enough to torment him as he lay dying slowly from his shot wound.

Amelia is a confident and gutsy character who will rise to any challenges thrown at her. She will turn situations around, transform mistakes into blessings. With the capability and intelligence to see things in different angles, she shares her somewhat blunt yet honest views with some aplomb.

Not only Mrs Bates accepted her faults, she admitted them disarmingly to her best friend, the wronged woman, Angela Wilton-Cough but also to the town's Doctor and the Priest. Together, they formed, unknown to Abraham Wilton-Cough, the small contingent that will protect and preserve the honour of both parties. All are extremely aware of the pride of Abraham which prevent him to just even acknowledge any of his wrong doings. They hatched a plan in order for the childless Amelia to be able to keep her unborn child in a fashion which does not destroy her reputation.

In the partly premonitory feverish dream of Wilton-Cough, we see the result of his infidelity with Mrs Bates, Abigail but also the one of the plan to let her be kept by Amelia.

The consequences of which made the Widow Bates own proudly an epitaph on her grave which states:

'Here, lay the sweetest and dearest of souls, Mrs Amelia Bates, born Elroy, February 1801, the adoptive mother of many orphans of Wilton Town, the biggest, largest and richest heart known in town until it passed away, blessed by all in August 1876.'

Transcending Amelia through her tiny mistake: it gave her finally her own family and more. Age thirty six at her first and last pregnancy, she had no desire to give up the child under pretence of respectability to the judging community of Wilton Town. Her confession to compassionate Father Odell made him work out a plot to save his about to be stoned sheep in his flock.

The fate of Amelia Bates provides smiles and hope aplenty. She is annoyingly enjoyable to be with and follow from grave to grave in the story.

Her character was born from observations. The clues are in the numbers. She is a very happy blend of about three real characters. Guess who?

Amelia Bates in quotes:

'The ancient skeletal woman, grabbed a pair of very old spectacles hidden within her bonnet, and putting them before her eyes sockets, advanced,

-Yes, it is very grand to have a name, the names of your forefathers and dates showing up after so many years in gold upon the marble, I must applaud at that

I suppose but they forgot to put something else, something meaningful about you, a eulogy. Did you leave nothing to be talked about between your birth date and the last one? Come and see my grave...'

'-Come you must regret one thing or two for we are all far from perfect and only human after all. Besides, making mistakes is part of life's learning curve. I have done a fair few in my time. The best mistake of all was our daughter, for example, which taught me never to regret some of my errors.'

'-Fiddlesticks! Let's meet him! If I didn't know you better, I would swear that you are slightly scared of him: your son is intimidating you, at long last. Tables do turn around once in a while frighteningly so. Do you remember dragging his young hand to that boarding school, to his new intimidating Head Master? Do you remember the constant beat of the ruler that teacher played upon his own hands while welcoming his new pupil? That ruler beat your son's palms to a pulp one day to that very same rhythm that is filling the air now. I think you cannot go back, Jo is acknowledging your presence by his musical welcome... Do you remember what you said to him in front of that Head Master? Let me refresh your memory and tell you exactly the same: Come on, man up!'

'-Because I made a point to know everything. For every matter that matters are close to my heart. Now there is only one way to beat fate my dear Abraham, so do not be defeated before it is all over for you. You have one hour to go and sixty minutes to make something out of them. The clock is ticking, the countdown has started. Come with me and keep listening to your heartbeat.'

Angela Wilton-Cough

Angela is the beautiful yet suffering wife of Abraham Wilton-Cough. Present by his death bed, she holds his hand until his last breath. She is the recipient of his last orders, the soldier that can execute his last will, which starts with burning the ones he had written previously with a lawyer and friend, with a cold and calculating heart: The very will which would have seen her become totally destitute and dying on the church steps of Wilton Town's church a very bitter winter night, the 23rd of January 1866.

Mrs Wilton-Cough is very much central and pivotal to the entire story, for she is the one who bestows the heart of Abraham. Daughter of an Italian shopkeeper, her marriage to Abraham Wilton-Cough is an advantageous one, putting her in the tight knit society of the descendants of the founders of Wilton Town. From being a guest and invited to parties, she can now hold them as a respected host. She becomes renown for her tea parties. She loves society and shines in the midst of many.

This last point makes Abraham uncomfortable. He constantly worries that Angela would attract the attention of a better man than him, who would be blown away by her beauty and intrinsic charm. If he consents to the tea parties at his home, under the false pretension of hating balls, dinners and large gatherings, he stops his couple from attending any of them. He jealously guards his wife at home by fear of losing her if she ventures out. His rather extreme lack of trust imposed upon Angela's shoulders is the mere reflection of his own lack of trust about his own self. His cynical self doesn't believe for one moment that Angela could possibly genuinely love him for himself. Abraham Wilton-Cough has a very low opinion of his own self and an acute knowledge that he is not the most amiable man. He hides this from all under the wrap of an overwhelming pride lined with a show of tyrannical confident authority.

The irony of Abraham's story is that Angela truly loved him. She fell for his pride associated with the confidence he displayed. The besotted wife of Wilton-Cough falls under his spell. His orders become rules written in an imaginary household book: this is how it is in the Wilton-Cough's home. He means to her, her entire life almost as if he was a god. Completely devoted to her husband, Angela is far from imagining her life without him or envisaging leaving him for someone else. A loving mother, straying is not on her mind at all, just the happiness of her children. If straying is not on the mind of Abraham either, he is the one who does it, once. After imposing such a reclusive lifestyle to his popular and well loved wife, it is Wilton-Cough who misbehaves under the influence of alcohol.

The guilt, knowing how he treated Angela the entirety of their wedded life, is enough to plague him on his death bed. His mistake, having a result in the Widow Bates being pregnant, breaks down the implacable defences tower that Abraham has built around him all his life. It is the simple fault which widens the gaps between every single brick to expose the individual behind it: a character, which was rather scared all along, yet covered himself with proud pretence to rule whatever he may or whoever he loved.

The bricks, the entire wall he has laid, the rules, his orders, thought like laws within his family, do not stack up together. They lack the consistency of cement to bind them together, or something strong called love. Wilton-Cough is a man who failed to show his love when he had time to do so.

Irony for irony, the loving Angela does the same. She fails to reassure her dying husband in his last minutes about her love for him. She is confessing so on deaf/dead ears.

Angela Wilton-Cough in death, in the nightmare, also shows her caricatured aspects. The centre of the tea party in her pauper's grave, she is her own woman who have seen tough days. The death of Abraham did mean poverty for her and her son Josiah. Yet she is that undefeated character who will keep the party going anyhow beyond the grave. Centre of attention of an eclectic mix of skeletons, all socialising, gossiping, she sets the trend like in her living past. Her decision on a peculiar tea, or even a digestive biscuit is regarded with due respect and followed by many. Angela, who gave the best of her life to a man who chose to ignore her mere existence in his will, felt her love trampled by a thousand heavy horses telling her that she had just been gold digging. In her grave, it is a rightly offended Angela that we meet. She knows everything from her own heart to the love affair of Abraham. She strongly chooses to ignore him in death.

Their beyond the grave encounter works like an eye for an eye punishment for Abraham. He admits all his wrong doing or almost to his wife, there and then, giving her his shrunken dry heart for all it is worth to keep or throw, for it belonged to her all along. Heartbreakingly, he leaves her grave and tea party having been completely ignored.

The lesson in Wilton-Cough's nightmare is learnt as when the character regains consciousness, his first actions are to ensure that his cold headed written will is destroyed to be replaced by a caring one. But also his words show finally consideration to his wife when he gives his final orders, wishes to her. He is conscious of having retrieved the Angela which he married, the one which he has not left yet by an untimely death, the one which has not lived a miserable and struggling existence after him, the one which has bravely endured living by his demeaning sides without an arguing word in reply, the patient soul which had accepted the like of him as a husband with so many kind and forgiving smiles that he could not count them on his death bed.

The Character of Angela is restored to her former self in the Erasing part of the story: she is the soldiering wife, ready to accept any order with almost blind love and blind respect. Unlike the Widow Bates, who has learnt to live without her husband for many years, who has taught herself to stand alone, and make her own stand anyhow, unlike Amelia who can tell how it is at her own doors at any point in time, who can correct anyone rather bluntly, disregarding their social status, Angela is a character that will conform to any rules, right or wrong. But she has a silent reply, one born out of forbearing love.

For example faced with the partiality her husband displays with their two sons, she is making sure the one left wanting has her support. Her last son, Josiah, and her developed a special bond, a strong one that help them go through adversity.

The 'Socialite' Angela sees the talent in Josiah as a pianist with the sheer glee of a proud parent straight away, and is ever so keen to promote him on his musical pursuit unlike the pragmatic Abraham who only sees a future impoverished church organist in his youngest son and tries to convince him to become a banker instead.

Angela Wilton-Cough only dares to defy her husband beyond the grave when it hurts the most, when everything is getting squared. Her life's silent forbearance will never be forgotten pass death point, the point of no return, when one has done whatever he/she wanted by will or not.

The creation of her first name was another mind given. Almost born from the onset. She is an Angel with a letter at the end: A: A the first letter that is spelling Amour (Love) in French, the first letter in the alphabet. She is the character that teaches what it is to love for eternity to Abraham.

Angela in quotes:

From her husband:

'-I remember the first time I saw your enchanting smile, it was at the tea party of my aunt Josephine and her very words to me: 'whatever you do Abraham, do not fall in love with the Italian shop keeper's daughter.' I disobeyed and did the right opposite, for I could not forget the beautiful raven black curls, the deep blue eyes like the ocean to dive into, the yellow buttercup dress spreading around you like the rays of the sun. Anytime I see you somewhere, it is like gasping a big breath of fresh air, like seeing the sun in spring after a long winter, like feeling finally vibrantly warm inside. I am sorry to have loved you badly, jealously.'

Her character bestows the last words of the story:

'When the long arm of the clock reached the thirteenth minute of the hour, it was all over, for Abraham Wilton-Cough had nothing left to say to the entire world having given his last breath. His tearful wife closed his eyelids tenderly and kissed his lips full of sorrow herself, confessing softly,

-I forgot to tell you that I loved you for your proud guts, not your wealth, my Ab, and now I love you for yourself, for eternity.'

Harry Bates.

Private Harry Bates is the quintessence of absent characters. Talked about, missed, grieved, his lack of presence, nonetheless affects the other characters in many ways. Like a missing link the life of Harry Bates can explain and shed light about the lives of others and their behaviours. Let's take the example of the always well informed Amelia Bates to illustrate the point. She has developed that trait of her character because of the military career of her husband. Harry is the determining factor behind a self taught Amelia who reads the newspaper to know if he is still alive, which part of the world he is located, which battles he faced, their results and consequences on the world and people, and trying desperately to guess when would he possibly be able to come back.

Harry Bates never returns to Amelia. He is killed in battle. His untimely departure to another world creates confusion to who are left behind. The night of his funeral, the grieving characters of the story are left to deal with the chaos of his definite, this time, eternal absence.

Private Bates symbolises order and a better world. He elevates the humble Amelia Elroy to take her to the better part of the town. Her place there is respectable yet far from ostentatious. She is the well liked poor neighbour. The soldier makes his couple just survive on his wages. The honour of his profession provides his wife with an aura of respect within the community of Wilton Town.

His death symbolises disorder and chaos: The one who was fighting bravely for a better world is no more to bring it about. All who mourns him, drink themselves senseless bringing chaos to their own worlds, right at their own doorsteps, at a loss. They make the little big mistake in the making which changes their futures for the better or the worst.

Private Bates first name choice is an homage to Prince Harry's military career. It is also a reference to Harry Potter, for her Harry has become the fantasy character of Amelia, invisible yet ever so present.

To the inspiring Harry, cheers...

Aunt Josephine Cough.

Briefly mentioned, she is the character which presents Angela to Abraham in one of her tea parties, warning him to not fall in love with the Italian shop keeper's daughter.

Aunt Josephine is the would be keeper of old generations and old fashions yet to still be in fashion herself and for her parties not to be obsolete, she has to invite the new generation which brings life to the old town and the like of Angela. Angela is like a mirror of herself in her younger years, an up and coming socialite to be watched.

We do not know about the good looks Josephine bestowed, yet she is a commending member of the Wilton-Cough family. Although she did not want the union of Abraham and Angela, she will be present at their wedding and making sure it is accepted by others. She is someone who understands the concept of falling in love. She accepts the consequences of it, partly because she was not allowed to do so herself.

She is a Cough through and through, showing the only thing left to her: the family pride. Her unmarried self does not condemned her nephew to wed Angela. She gives the couple a beautiful cuckoo clock from her lonely trips as a wedding present.

That dainty object with its repetitive sounds is disliked with a passion by Abraham who can not stand it, yet for the love of his wife who likes it, he accepts it in their bedroom. The cuckoo clock ticks his unrest as he sleeps. It plays as a fateful object which marks Wilton-Cough's last minutes. Abraham was the cuckoo in his own nest destroying it at every stroke, hour and minute.

In his last moments, he can not ignore the sound of the cuckoo clock which spells out his time of the day, his time in his life.

Aunt Josephine stands as a strong character who melts with time like everyone else by the never ending, timeless, strike of love.

Josiah Wilton-Cough.

Josiah by his imaginary piano/organ/organic instrument, playing beautifully and powerfully, is a pure vision. The youngest son of Abraham Wilton-Cough symbolises all the children who had to endure the will of their parents as their own. If they do not do so, they end up beaten up badly.

Yet Josiah has the power to make his father face the music beyond his grave: A tune played that returned to your ears, like the strike of a ruler on your hands, it is sharp and hurt enough to make you ponder: were you right to impose your own will on your child?

The nightmare part of the story highlights what became of Josiah. He is a ghost hence a restless soul. He loves and is loved, followed by a herd of other ghosts, he is commending in his own right. Buried at cross roads, with a simple slate marking his grave, hanged for murder, Josiah Wilton-Cough stands as a formidable and terrifying character with a dramatic past. He has reasons to be angry with almost the world, and in particular his father.

The bullied child becoming a pauper with his mother had to learn to use his fists for their protection on the streets of Wilton Town. Fallen on hard times, it is the friendship of prostitutes that make them get by to survive. Over the years, well acquainted with street laws, Josiah offers his protection to the prostitutes of the town. It is while saving one of them that he kills her assailant. This precipitated his arrest and murder conviction. After his hanging, the desolate Angela lives once more on the streets, where she dies miserably on the steps of a church during a cold winter.

The tragic story of the pathetic life of his youngest son who had kept looking after his mother until his death affects Abraham Wilton-Cough greatly. As a father, he realises that his own guilt goes much deeper than just his incapacity of understanding and appreciating the sensitivity and talent of his child. He had deprived Josiah of his proper love and care. He had even stripped his son from the affection and attention of his mother by throwing him far from the family home in a boarding school. His intentions were clear: toughen up the little boy.

From the fear that Angela would spoil Josiah into pursuing his dreams of becoming an artist, a pianist, Abraham cut them from his fortune in his cool headed, cold hearted last will. He leaves everything to his eldest who he had raise to be like him. His partiality is a blow hard to digest in the mist of his family for it is the one that breaks it apart.

Meeting the ghostly Josiah in the wood clearing he haunts, Abraham Wilton-Cough faces the results and consequences his strong convictions and actions had upon others. If he wanted his youngest to be tough, he is. He had to be, forced by circumstances beyond his power.

Josiah's character bestows strength grown from a miserable life in the streets protecting his mother and receiving the charity of a morsel of bread given by the escort girls living on the pavement. From being on the receiving end of charity to becoming one who the hopeless can turn to for protection and a home, giving them respect, paying back their helping hands with all his might, Josiah developed into Jo.

Either way, Jo or Josiah has the charisma that draws crowds to him. Let it be his talent to play the piano so dramatically well, let it be his great capacity to love women and understand their plight like no others can, he is a surrounded character just like his mother. Beyond his grave, he is still loved, remembered and respected as the resident ghost of the woods. Despite his hanging, all defend his memory, and all respect his voice.

From a wee child who impressed the ladies at the tea parties of his mother, who compared him to what they knew, the church organist, to become a dreaded ghost that haunts the wood by Wilton Town with his impressive music, Josiah still plays his own tune whatever is thrown at him.

From the nightmare back to his own dying reality, Abraham

changes his tune regarding his youngest. From a destroyer of his dreams, he corrects the situation to become his 'beyond the grave supporter', giving the acceptance of his uniqueness, Josiah needs and lacks.

Josiah Wilton-Cough in quotes:

'Slamming his closed fists upon his clavier, the ghost gave an incendiary glance at his father as he said sternly,

-I have no father. Mine passed away, dead and buried, he is best forgotten. He was a miserable man who made a point of ignoring my mum and I's mere existences. It past the point of no return. It was sealed with his grave. What is left are only memories of a dreadful individual who should rot in his tomb undisturbed for the peace and sake of everyone else.'

'Devastated, lonely, Abraham Wilton-Cough walked towards his grave lost in his sad thoughts when he saw his son's ghost Josiah followed by his ghostly girls upon the same wild path heading towards his mother's pauper's ditch. Moving sideways to let the ghosts past, the skeleton stood there silently hoping not to be recognised, nor noticed for he remembered what Mrs Bates had said about the dead being dismantled. His wishes were not granted as he saw the imposing figure of Jo stopping right by him and asking,

-Do I know you from somewhere, skeleton? Lift your skull a little so I can see you properly under the moonlight.

Frightened Abraham obeyed taking a good glance at his son as he replied, keeping his hat close to his chest,

-You do know me, Josiah. I am your father, the one that is very sorry for everything he did or almost.

Smiling cruelly to him, Jo crossed his strong muscled shadowy arms upon his chest, repeating like if he was tasting the very word within his lips,

-Almost... What could you possibly not be sorry for my dear father?'

In Abraham's words:

'-Let me tell you that the very first time I held you in my arms and saw the same blue eyes as Angela staring at me, I was far from sorry for my actions then, I was very proud of the result of one to say the least.'

Noah M Wilton.

Noah M Wilton is the revered character, founder of Wilton Town, ancestor of Abraham Wilton-Cough. We hear about him first, mentioned proudly by Abraham who boast to be the eleventh removed from him.

Larger than life, Noah takes shape and form in a formidable statue in the delirious dying dream of Wilton-Cough. As Abraham catches his breath at the base of the colossal brass effigy of his ancestor, he regains stock of who he is, who he came from but also the courage to face his own future, hence the judgement for his mistakes.

Despite being a beacon, the founder of a town, Noah is far from being without faults himself. There are dark corners in his legacy which plagues his descendants like a curse. The foundation of the town was not easy. From the wilderness, out of the beaten track where Noah and his followers settled, they did not get many returns at first. In desperation, as famine took them one by one in a deadly toll, they started to eat their own dead to survive. From the disturbed graves of the eaten came the curse of their unrest upon who gets to live and have descendants. The curse is the monster within your family which you can barely tackle for it has grown out of proportion without your understanding. Every 150 years, descendants of the survivors, if born during a full moon night will be plagued by the curse of the eaten dead: they become ghouls. Without the necessity of their forefathers, they consume human flesh. Their grisly acts perpetrate upon all descendants of the first settlers in Wilton Town a form of punishment: none shall be allowed to rest in peace, as their ancestors disrespected their dead.

We found the dead of Wilton Town rising one Autumnal night, in Wilton-Cough's nightmare for in their peculiar town with its peculiar past, it is common currency yet the living are unaware of that fact that is until the day they pass away... There are more stories to come from the cemetery of that small town, like the first one, they will be published for every Halloween, ghosts and ghouls permitting.

Returning to our bold Noah, his character does not take simple measures. He is a strong fighter which will cut the mustard in any place in the world. He will survive and make you do so too with methods that may leave you pale and asking the internal question, if there were no other ways to get by. However he lifts the spirits of many by his sheer engagement to deal and tackle what no one would and be left beaten by.

Like his namesake, he is one that gets to resettle upon Earth. He saved as many as he can doing so. He is the tough decision maker that all turn to. Passed away, his legacy remains strong. Passed away, he gets to stand tall in a living statue, brass shining, axe swirling, arse kicking. His metaphorical self will always make it through and make sure others following his footsteps do just as well.

Regarded by all as an heroic figure, almost a legendary one, his lineage bestows the consideration of everyone as being important. Although Noah had humble origins being born from a peasant couple, he displayed leadership qualities from an early age. He became a logger in order to provide his parents with a better roof. However the hardship of being tenants felt throughout the village meant that no one could ever hope to raise on day above poverty. The cruelty of the owner of the land of his parents grew to such an extent that the young Noah plotted for all hit hard by the imposed extreme taxes to escape to uncharted land, still free for all to claim.

The sheer charisma of Noah M Wilton made him be followed by the entire village with not one soul missing. The story of Noah, his followers and the creation of Wilton Town will be narrated in a fairy tale like novel... Watch this space.

Noah M Wilton in quotes:

'This must be his last straw, he thought. However a strong voice and hand recalled him,

-Abraham, stand up and face everything. You are one of mine hence strong.

On your feet now.'

'Seizing the chin of the skeleton, the statue of Noah revealed,

-This very town was founded by eating our own dead. This is what we had to do to survive. Some of our descendants are since plagued to become ghouls. The fate of Zachary is not your fault, it is entirely mine. Let me deal with your bone suckers. Join the others and wait for your own judgement.

Doing as he was told, Abraham Wilton-Cough saw the colossal brass statue of his ancestor stepping down from its base and brandishing his huge axe against the incoming ghouls. It resounded like the clashes of the titans with gunshots hitting metal and the vibrant noise of the battle axe against flesh and bones. The living dead were literally hacked off Wilton Town by its very founding father.'

Father Odell.

The character of Father Odell looks after his parish like a shepherd after his flock. Ready listener of their ailments and tribulations, he offers to them the comfort of an educated comprehension, wraps their shoulders by his understanding and instead of letting them face their worst nightmare alone, he leads them to forgiving solutions to their dilemmas.

Father Odell, far from throwing the first stone to someone confessing to him their misdeeds, offers them the protection of his forgiving help and secrecy. He would also stand to protect them from public judgement depending on their deeds in order to fulfil what he believes, that only god is allowed to judge someone fairly and adequately. He aims for his sheep to have a lifetime where they could redeem themselves before facing god.

Theo Odell believes that humanity can earn their colours in the end, yet he will stand against mass mob judging, stoning and murders. 'You shall not kill': is the rule in his heart. When you do so you become a murderer in the eyes of the eternal father and there is nothing worst. Father Odell will protect his flock from becoming 'all judging' murderers.

His character brings back forgiveness into religion rather than the gun blazing extremism which we face today in all shapes or forms. Asked for your own religion, you face a bullet in your head by your reply, depending where you stand at that moment in time. We are facing religious and ethnic cleansing on a massive scale. Some believe they have a right to kill you for your differing faith. Some are inhuman enough to do so for a religious political tyranny which they want to expand worldwide at all cost, humanity's one.

Theo is the accomplice that will carry you through a phase of history and make sure you are left alive. I based him upon one of my own ancestors, Julie Postel, known as Ste Marie-Madeleine Postel from her canonisation. A teacher in the small village of Barfleur, she helped priests, hide and cross to Great Britain, where they would not be beheaded for their religion, during the French revolution years.

Theo's name was born from the singer of 'Another Love', which I listened to a lot during the time when I wrote 'Hair raising, Heir Rising, Erasing.'. For me it meant the greater love, the pure one, the humanistic one which embraced everybody in its scope.

This character will come back in my stories of Wilton Town.

In one protective quote:

'The priest intervened at the bitterness of the comments,

-Abraham, maybe it would be best for your sons to step away now before you confess everything to everyone. Have you said your farewells to them?'

Terah Wilton-Cough.

Father of Abraham Wilton-Cough, Terah is just mentioned by him with great pride. This character is not elaborated in this story.

From the association of two powerful families, the Wiltons and the Coughs, Terah is a member of the third generation. His important wealth handed down to his son made him own half of Wilton Town. Still not enough, Abraham endeavoured to increase his fortune by creating the first bank of the town.

Terah married a Cough, the sister of aunt Josephine, Juliette. Juliette, like her sister was a renown beauty in her days. If we do not know in this story, the childhood Abraham bestowed with Juliette as a mother and Terah as a father, if it is not mentioned, I can however reveal that it was pretty much a loveless family. Abraham is the only child of the couple. Blamed by his mother for ruining her figure and her happier partying days, he is given to the care of nannies then sent and forgotten about in a boarding school. Aunt Josephine is the only one who picks up occasionally her nephew for his school holiday.

If the unremarkable child, Abraham is, is refused the entry to the drawing room when his mother is entertaining guests, he is accepted as an important guest by his own aunt to her tea parties.

Where was Terah? He was hunting. Living from his abundant territory and tenants, Terah was a man who lost his interest in his wife and her beauty almost as soon as she fell pregnant. His little boy did not interest him either: Abraham was meek and far from a physically strong boy that could follow in his hunts without crying from a tear in his pants to watching a deer dying and butchered.

Terah had no care in the world apart his passion for hunting and guns. Juliette had no care in the world apart her own self and the attention she got from a string of lovers. From his background, Abraham Wilton-Cough can be better understood, his actions, his intrinsic fears, his bitterness.

What Terah represented to Abraham was a strong masculine figure, he admired but could not mimic positively. He was no hunter, yet knew his guns and how to handle one because of Terah, although this failed to protect him when faced by one in the midst of his own bank.

Terah's character gave the pride of the Wilton-Cough to Abraham but also the legacy of a faltering family life which was pretty much denied, or non-existent.

Following his bad example or not, the main character was defined by his father's attitude to everything.

The first name of Abraham's father was inspired by his biblical namesake. His false idols which drive him out of love are his guns.

Doctor Valdi.

Doctor Vincent Valdi is another character barely mentioned in the story. At the bedside of the dying Abraham Wilton-Cough, he is monitoring his last hours, unable to save him.

Like Angela Wilton-Cough and Amelia Bates, he is from the generation of people who came to make their lives in Wilton Town. Well regarded, Doctor Valdi is an indispensable member of the community. He is present at the birth of its people and at their death. Best friend of father Theo Odell, the atheist Valdi shares with him the passing and going of all in Wilton Town. He also beholds the secrets of everyone in town like the priest does. The two men serve as watcher and peacekeeper of Wilton Town population.

They settle dispute among themselves before they even arise in the open in town: like how to make sure Mrs Bates does not end up stoned by her peers in her shameful condition? They put charity and forgiveness into action first and foremost. They care about lives in tandem.

Wherever Valdi has trodden to save a life, Father Odell will follow suit, called by him to bring comfort to a departing soul.

Like his counterpart, Doctor Valdi will be back in my stories of Wilton Town.

Zachary Wilton-Cough

What can I say about Zach? The first time you encounter him you will not like him a tad. I wrote him with his sheer stupidity aligned with his false cleverness. Zachary Wilton-Cough is a character as daunting as a sponge which was left to absorb vitriol until it is so poisonous, your guts instinct are to just leave it there and ran away without dealing with it or squeeze it out of the bullshit it is full of.

What can I say about Zachary? His first name starts by a Z, unlike his father. He symbolises the end of the alphabet, the end of culture, the end of love. Zach poses as a dreary dead end, the final error of an answer which no one wants.

What can I say about that ghoul? He was a child, loved and cherished. His father prioritised him above all else, left him his entire fortune (in the nightmare) yet it doesn't explain the way he turns out to be.

When his own father found him plundering his grave, he fails to understand his son for he had given everything to him. Yet Abraham will not get any respect for whatever he gave. Zach is soulless, heartless, materialistic to the core. Zach can eat his own parents without remorse. He became a ghoul.

How to discuss with Zach in his state is an impossibility. He is a killer with a gain and aim which render your murder negligible compared to his fast feasting reward with your bones.

Of course Zachary is a metaphor for the worst, we encounter in our century. Explained or not, Zach is a threat which will cull without a reasoning heart, swearing to whoever, just mass murdering.

Zachary is a brainwashed fool, a ghoul, a killer: no longer a son, nor a human. Zachary meets a deadly end, the one he gave to many. However we will meet him again as his ghostly father will haunt the living in order to save his eldest son from becoming a ghoul, desperately seeking to lift the curse of Wilton Town.

Zach in quotes:

'Trying to fix up the part of his flapping scalp, Zachary winked at his father with a cocky smirk as he answered,

-I am not too worried for them two, for the less we are the more we feast. Apart for that missing bit of brain now don't you think I look dashing and very well preserved, dad? I will let you into our little secret to great longevity: we eat people dead or alive, the fresher the better.

Stepping away from his son, seized by an uncontrollable shiver, Abraham was in total disarray. It dawned on him that Zachary Wilton-Cough went through his tomb: was he looking to eat his very own father? He pointed to his grave shakily then to himself repetitively a few times wanting explanations, demanding,

-Do I truly look like a happy meal to you?

Turning around his father ever so slowly, considering him as meat for the grab, making Abraham tremble of fright doing so, Zachary finally stated,

-Not as very well conserved as I expected, I am afraid. I thought your money would have bought a decent coffin with tin like quality attached to it. Yet I am very much mistaken, you are pretty much rotten all over. Your bones might still make perfect toothpicks for dirty nachos.

The terrifying Zach went to pick up a piece of Abraham's rib that laid flat at his feet from the shooting, and put it in his mouth to illustrate his point. Then he showed a silver flask of whiskey, waving it slightly to his old man, before commenting with his brightest grin, and licking his purple lips,

-When I thought this little silver baby with it's vintage golden content was the most precious thing I could grab from your grave, I come to the realisation that your good old bones taste like cheese straws so full of marrow they are.

Calling out his companions at once, Zachary Wilton-Cough shouted, pointing at his father,

-Guys! Snack time! Cheese straw bones down here!

Forgetting his intentions to pick up all his pieces of shattered bones within his top hat at once, Abraham legged it out of there as fast as he could.'

Wilton Town.

Wilton Town is a whimsical place with a far-West feel to it. Created out of the sheer wilderness of a large, dark and strange forest by the broad axe of Noah M Wilton, it represents all the hope of a better future that people do carry with them. However it didn't quite synthesise itself on the ground, despite Noah and his followers's best will and efforts. The hard working and generous Noah provided them with the free land, built the houses, designed a small town out of the treasure of their surrounding seas of trees.

First of all, they nearly all failed to understand the new ecosystem they had disturbed by their sudden presence. The belief that they could grow the same crops that they did before, where they came from, was soon dispelled into a famine which lasted as long as they took to learn to a point perfect their new territory. Hunting provided some food to survive however hit by a succession of hard winters, the newly established community dwindled rapidly to a handful of men and women left.

Sheer hunger made them do the unthinkable: they dug up their dead to eat. It made them survive at a cost: Wilton Town was cursed. In the following stories about this little town you shall learn who put a terrible spell on its survivors. Their descendants, all affected by the curse, faces unrest. Only a fair few remain undisturbed in the cemetery of Wilton Town. RIP is not widely known in this town.

The dead are alive with the sound of music. They rise from their graves. They come to terms with whatever they have to and if they are lucky they will not end up eaten by a ghoul which more often than not are their own sons and daughters. Welcome to Wilton Town...

Finding It-666: the Beast.

It-666's story can not be told in one sentence not even in one book. It has a fateful spin to it which will last for as long as it is meant to last. It is determined.

Let me confess, it feels strange to even speak about It or mention her. 'It' came knocking on my imagination's door via nightmares that would not go away, that would get repeatedly spookier by the night, so much so that I would sit and stare at the four walls of my own bedroom with all lights on, too afraid to just sleep. Thank god, I did not have a partner at that time. He would have thought I went bonkers. I thought I did go so myself until I started writing what I saw in those nightmares.

It made me stop the flow of 'Clementine Boatswain's adventures in the After world', her blog, and her five books out of eleven in full swing (that work is unpublished but on the map of future publication). Just like that, one summer, many sleepless nights, I had the urge to write It out of my body/soul/spirit/psyche. With saddle bags under my eyes, I wrote about 'It'. 'Clementine' is still at a stand still to this day but I intend to return to her, at some point, finish her adventures, eleven books, with a prequel which just had to be and two sequels which are happy endings.

As I lay 'It' down on paper, my nightmares about her decreased. I am still disturbed to described them fully. It was as if I was in a Being which could not speak properly, which would not defend itself but had the might to do so and was put to slaughter. I started writing about 'It' after one distressingly bad dream, where I was crucified upside down in my own bedroom. It felt so real that I was confused in the morning. Morning, still in bed, no holes in any parts of my body, just a bloody dream, AGAIN. I did check myself throughout but also that I was not surrounded by walls bleeding tears of blood.

The character of It was awake, alive, stuck in a cage somewhere and had to be rescued. Her story flowed from me to the point where the sleepless nights were not due to nightmares anymore but just writing It/it. I am a bit of a workaholic when it comes to creative writing. It is hard for me to stop. I have penned four books of the It-666 saga with a fifth on the map. All are at different stages of publication. The first one is published, the second back from the proof reader, the third and fourth to be sent to the proof reader.

The saga starts with 'Finding It-666: the Beast.' During the Fall of 2012, Private Investigator, Walter Workmaster stumbled across a tortured teenager kept in a cage under a pentagram in a bunker. Saving 'It' turns the atheist world of Workmaster upside down...

Let's meet the characters.

It-666, the Beast.

We meet 'It' at the start of the saga, aged 16, in an appalling state. Kept in a cage, starved, tortured, left in her own mess, the teenager has only one wish, the one of dying. Representing all we fear, the incarnated Beast, is a young distressed Being. She had far from the most enjoyable start in life.

Found by Walter Workmaster, she is surprised to see his human reaction to her. She is met with his heartbroken sympathy and his desire to help her out. His friendly humanity touches her deep down. Despite seeing her mark, the atheist rejects the fact that she could possibly be the Beast and treats her like an individual in great need of help. Despite her confessing to him that she is a freak, he takes her on board of his family life like a Super Being of some sort and pushes others to treat her like so.

Literally adopted by the human, the teenage Beast discovers hope but also that she may be allowed to have a future. It is hard for herself to comprehend that she may live for her hurting heart is casting repetitively death for her own self. The suicidal creature that she is, her tortured soul who has difficulties in coming to terms that she is the feared Beast, absolutely doesn't want to hurt anyone nor be used to destroy humanity. She would rather pass away than letting that happen. Knowing that she is a living bundle of extreme powers which she doesn't know how to control fully, she lives in fear of causing the worst. She contemplates her suicide as the kindest thing she could do to others.

However, saved by Workmaster, he drives her straight, unknowingly to her incarnated counterparts, Angels and Archangels, which have been walking the earth for an eternity, mixing with and protecting humans in a well kept secret. The first she meets Archangel Gabriel assesses her. Taken aback by her gentle character and pacific nature, he takes her under his wings, knowing that if others find out about her existence, she will either be slaughtered or used and abused to do evil. Despite his own best effort to keep the Beast only known, hidden and protected by him and Workmaster, the news inevitably reaches the leader of the incarnated Angels, his fearsome Uncle, Archangel Raphael.

From her encounter with Gabriel, It cannot help a strong bond forming between them which develops into the deepest love. The Beast simply falls for the Archangel irresistibly. Thought at first to be just a teenage crush, all watch helplessly the union establishing itself between the two Beings.

With her case being overwhelmingly pleaded by Walter Workmaster, but also because of her strong good self sacrificing heart, she wins over Raphael and his Angels. The Archangel gives her a chance and takes her in the midst of his Angelic Army as a soldier.

From a lost Being with no confidence about herself and others, she grows to accept herself but also learns that her powers can be used to do good. From training, participating in Angelic missions, and fighting with the Army against demons, she acquires a particular place among Beings.

She is allowed to live and grow in the safe knowledge that the day she turns evil, the Angels surrounding her, will give her the death she wants to protect humanity.

The Beast is a complex character, not only evolving, but growing in a lot of respect. Young, sweet sixteen, she has a lot to learn as a supernatural Being, as a teenager who was deprived of a proper childhood, who spent part of it feral in the Black Forest where a priest and a nun hid her after abducting her at birth, and the rest of it in a cage, regularly tortured, and as a powerful creature who finally meet some acceptance from others. She also grows on the other characters irresistibly. She doesn't have to play the charm incentive to do so: she is just her natural self.

She is the antithesis of what or who she is supposed to be. Self-sacrificing soldier, she meets respect and admiration, the more she engages in missions, fights and battles. Throughout, there is the fear, the danger that she could be too good to be true, and that all are learning to trust pure evil in a sheep skin's disguise. Is it a clever move to teach Angelic warfare to your possible enemy? Some could argue with a 'keep your friends close and your enemy closer.' Aren't Her Angelic Watchers learning how the little Beast fights by training her? The question of trust is one of the main theme within the saga, investigated in many of its different aspect.

A dangerously restrained character, It has the potential to bring complete chaos yet she doesn't do so when we encounter her. All (characters and readers alike) meet a rather sweet Being, brave, steadfast in her will to cause no hurt to others. As the Beast, however, a considerable amount of positively negative experiences are thrown at her, time and time again. How strong can a character be to not switch and explode once and for all?

The first instalment of her saga is all about her discovered self-destroying tender Being, adopted by a kind and open minded human, taken under the wings of a rather aloof yet inquisitive Archangel Gabriel but also her taking the potentially dangerous offer of being raised by the Angels in their Army.

I fear I have said too much and not enough about 'It'. Let's correct that a tad.

In the balance, on the too much side:

'It-666' has to be one of the most heavyweight characters, I ever created. When characters present themselves to my mind gradually or not, they rather feel like imaginary friends. I dwell upon them, see them acting and from a virtual director's chair, ask them to repeat something once more with more passion. Disturbingly, I felt in It's shoes. Now, she had dirty branded bare foot that she could not move from the layer of her own piss and shit she was sitting upon, cramped, dislocated in parts, bruised, with too many broken bones to be spoken of. From my nightmares, It felt deep down physically, like if I was within her, living her hardships. Writing her story helped me step away from 'It' all, like if I was removing her skin from my shoulders, breathing awake as normal. It was like releasing a white feathered dove from her cage and letting her fly to freedom: a relief.

On the not enough side:

Experiencing a character that way was a novelty as a creative mind: disturbing, definitely yes, enlightening just as much. However faced with the choice to carry a novel with the vision from the deep end, or else, I selected else: Else, the other characters that encounter the Beast and what they make of It. Let's emphasise: What they are making of It, the teenage Being they decided to bring up together.

How will it turn out is the big question. I will let you read it in due course.

How would the Beast (well my It) look like on an identity card or passport:

Country of origin: UK.

Born in London the 06/06/1996 at 6:16 am.

Surname: 666.

First Name: It.

Given Names: Bambi, Blondie.

Nationality: Being of some kind. Gender: F Height: when humanly incarnated: 1,53m. In Beast's shape: undisclosed.

Residence: The tree house of Doctor Gabriel Purallee. (Archangel Gabriel)

Colour of eyes: Aquamarine.

Under the Guardianship of: her three Angelic Masters and Watchers: Archangel Raphael, incarnated as Raphael Wrath; The Death Angel, incarnated as Azryel Mortimer; Archangel Gabriel, incarnated as Dr Gabriel Purallee.

Birth Father: Fallen Archangel Eremiel.

Birth Mother: Demonic Goddess Lilith.

Adoptive Father: Walter Workmaster.

Adoptive Mother: Caroline Workmaster, born Purallee.

The born Beast is a sensitive Being with feelings bursting at her every pore. She was not offered proper sympathy nor love of a filial kind until she meets the wonder of a human that is Walter Workmaster...

It-666 in quotes (from Book 1) and passages:

'It-666 smiled and softly told,

-I have no avenging thirst, Gabriel. Making sure they didn't know that I had dangerous powers, implied either laying low or using them to destroy all who thought I had, and a carnage doing so. I prefer being destroyed than using my powers or being used and abused to do evil. Here I am all broken up for it, to preserve humanity from all I can do. And my vow not to harm anyone stands proud and tall, renewed for having seen only one man, Walter, opening his arms to me, with genuine kindness, taking me away from my hell spot upon Earth. I can swallow any pain given, as for kindness I want to give it back tenfold. I read that Walter was not a happy man, he is hurting. I want to help him if I can. Repay him for the hope he gave me.'
(verse 9: Of rats and men.)

'Gabriel who broke the news of the abduction to a distraught Caroline and Workmaster, turned at the mention of his name. He walked forward to the group of Angels surrounding the young Beast, and knelt before Azryel Mortimer bowing his head down,

-I accept. Help us forward. Help us retrieve young Michael. My failures are calling for guidance to correct my path. Only your intransigence Azryel can drive back a soldier to his best.

It-666 gave her solemn reply to Raphael and his Death Angel,

-My Master has spoken. I bow to you both, Azryel servant of Archangel Raphael. What is the plan to get back Archangel Michael? What can I do to help?

Raphael replied with glowing eyes,

-Just fight with Us Bambi, just fight.'
(verse 27: Greet & Meet/Great & Meat.)

'Great light poured into the room, as Azryel and It-666 materialised within it. Raphael glanced at them worryingly yet before he could say one word, he saw the young teenage Beast walk to the bedside of Micky. She enclosed both of his wrists between her hands and whispered a reversed incantation. Before their eyes the child's deep cuts sealed themselves closed. She kissed his forehead gently, saying,

-You will sleep now and forget about it all, Micky, for it was all a bad, very bad dream. You are safe. It is all over like mummy said.

The child blinked a little then fell asleep, safe, sound, and healed up. Raphael picked up his little hand and checked his wrist thoroughly, assessing the child's bodily functions doing so, he confirmed to Caroline,

-Micky is going to be more than fine. He will not remember what he lived and saw. Nothing happened but school today for him, now. He does not need any intervention from any healing Angels regarding his blood loss either, for right now it is fully re-established. Caro, your child has just been healed thoroughly by It.

Caroline fell inside her uncle's arms and cried,

-Thank you, thank you all for bringing him back, for tending to him, for healing him, thank you so much. I am indebted to you.

Azryel came to check the child as Raphael did, but more thoroughly so. He nodded his confirmation to Raphael and Caroline. Micky was healed, safe and sound.

As he glanced back at It-666, she was far from alright. He could see both her wrists bleeding slowly. She had swallowed the pain and the ordeal of the child and took it upon her. 'Swallowing Pain' was one attribute of the Beast but a dangerous one. The digestion of pain was a process very much unknown to many Angels and the ultimate result could mean worse than what was absorbed. Death looked worryingly at Raphael and told,

-I have one soldier to tend to, I am afraid.'
(verse 30: Re-Cove-Ry.)

Walter Workmaster.

I must say before I even start talking about him, I am fond of Walter who earned himself many nicknames from Wreck-Man to the shit-stirrer. If the character was alive and real, I would take him to the pub and go for a long 'talking shit over pints' session, reviewing whatever happened that week from news to politics passing by a glimpse on our love lives and see where they are at, eager to ear what he had to say about everything.

Walter Workmaster is a man, a human, imperfect like one. He sweats, shouts, swears yet cares so much and generously loves others to stand as their spokes person to defend and protect them. Not afraid of punching someone down for you, he is a lively character who anyone finds hard to make him shut up or to not listen to.

The character faced a massive break down when his twin sister Wendy passed away, years earlier before we meet him in 2012. His break down was bad enough to be etched in the minds of all who witnessed it or heard of it. It created 'Wreck-Man' or the myth of him. It ruptured his marriage, with his wife leaving him, frightened for his sanity, only thinking of protecting their two year old son. The separation sent the man further down in a spiralling depression.

The helping hand, which took him away from the brink of a suicidal death was the one of his brother in law, Gabriel Purallee. They have a very special brotherly bond, yet a tough one. They do not take any shit from one another, or it seems like it, for they are always there for each other. When Walter loves Caroline, Gabriel's younger sister, Big Gab loved Wendy Workmaster and was betrothed to her when she died. The two are just pure family. The baseball bat joke is just a symbol of their love and hate relationship. They have been together through a lot and will see each other through no matter what.

Divorced from Caroline, not by his own choice, Walter is not only unable to rebuild a life with someone else, he doesn't even consider it. He loves his Caro. Back from his brink and break down, being able, allowed to see his son, spending some afternoons with him and seeing a little Caroline in doing so, makes his days and keeps him going. The separation devastated him to the point that Walter had lost all confidence and self esteem.

Gabriel took charge of the broken man that Walter was for four long years in his house in the wood before he trusted him to live on his own again. In 2012, at the start of the story, Workmaster had been in his own flat for a couple of years. He is also at a moment in his life where he is taking steps to reform himself. He quit smoking and has started to quit drinking for about a week. However he does not harbour the hope that cleaning up his act would bring him back Caroline. The character doesn't think very highly of himself.

But others do. For a start his son, Michael, nicknamed, Micky adores and admires his father. He is eager to listen and gather the advice of his well educated dad. Full of wisdom, Workmaster is an excellent father, cherishing every minute he gets to see his son like if it was his last. The character has that internal fear that someone, Caro, Gab, anyone, would find him unfit again and deprive him of his child.

Although Caroline did split with him, she still loves him and does harbour a strong regret about the divorce. She does question her own actions when she faced the break down of Walter and in hindsight truly think that she should have staid with her husband and give him support in his hours of need. Yet she flew away from her conjugal nest with her son, only making the matter all the worse. She secretly blame herself to have made of Walter, the broken man that he is now. Devoted to her son and work, she does not consider rebuilding her life with someone else. She feels for the humbleness, the shyness of Walter around her. She remembers better days fondly and the man that wowed her.

The Walter Workmaster of the past was a brilliant law student who courted her effortlessly. He had that charisma, and the matching wild energy that she possessed. From student protests to demonstrations, she would follow him anywhere. Her ultimate accolade that she was dating him properly came as she presented him to her dotting yet daunting uncle Raphael.

Raphael Wrath brought up the orphaned Gabriel and Caroline. He had a soft spot for the wild Caroline to the extent that no one would ever be good enough for his niece. Walter and Wrath didn't see eye to eye, with one thinking of the other as a multi millionaire mobster and the other as a shit stirring student.

Their kind of father in law/son in law relationship if strained, grows and develops through time to mutual appreciation, respect to the point of conspiring together on future plans. The arrival on the scene of the young Beast irremediably pushes those two characters in the vicinity of each other where they move on from their hate and love relationship. The Archangel that is Raphael is actually very fond of Walter Workmaster and has been secretly involved to make sure, he was kept out of trouble many times. He considers the man as part of his family and as such is rather protective of him.

Walter Workmaster went on to become a successful Human rights lawyer. His cases, his stance, his work caused the admiration of many from his Caroline who was only too eager to be asked in marriage by him, to the Angels who were watching almost every step of that human.

Until the perfect world of Workmaster went crumbling down, until his twin sister Wendy was murdered, until he became known by his family and friends as Wreck-Man.

Turned Private Investigator, scraping a living together, the character at the start of the saga although reformed goes through everything in order to bring to justice the murderer of Wendy. This leads him to the bunker in the wood belonging to the politician Paul Peterson. This is where he makes the devastating discovery of the Beast. Touched by her plight, he frees that new victim of Peterson.

The almost legendary chaotic behaviour of the atheist that is Walter, is dreaded by all: what will they have to deal with to tidy up

the mess that Workmaster created?
None expected him to find the Beast and plead for her. Let alone to adopt her with the firm intention to bring her up and give her a little bit of a descent life and childhood back.

The character of Workmaster has a warm, generous and kind heart who understands what it is to be down and under. When none would give consideration, he would be the last man standing to bring you some, not only that to try to desperately turn the situation around. The character is the staunch advocate of It-666.

From their mutual understanding grows a strong filial affection between the human and the powerful Being. It trusts Walter completely, not only that, she would protect him with her life. Just by being himself, Workmaster makes the Beast love humanity. Walter develops further the contradiction that It-666 already is. The Angels can only make the constatation that it was the right man at the right time who found the Beast, and all partake of that human's dream that scripture can be rewritten, remastered, but also that it doesn't have to end with an apocalypse.

Writing Walter Workmaster is a sheer pleasure. Not often wrong, his words have the power to sway, convince, or simply be listened to with care. That particular human's rants are the food for thought for Raphael and his Angels. Far from being dismissed as non sense by them, Walter has become a human allowed in their incarnated walking the Earth secrecy. Raphael admits him as parts of his Beings' circles although he is only human. Walter bestows a VIP status among Angel. Throughout the saga, we learn why it is the case. Just to let you know, the preceding bio of the character is only the tip of the iceberg of Walter Workmaster.

His status is not due to his good looks. Imagine a man who does not care for one moment for his appearance and you will see Walter: Dusky blue eyes, an untamed blond mop which has a length which could qualify it as a mane, a chin not regularly free of hair, baggy shirt open onto a Tee shirt of some sort that we never know when it was last cleaned or changed, upon jeans usually riped from his treks and quests in woods and sewers. He is a man on a hunt, the one that will bring down the politician who killed his sister, and looks like a hunter which tracked his deer in the forest for days without a rest. Caroline's nickname for him is 'Blondie Bear'. In his heyday, Walter didn't have that un-kept appearance, nonetheless even with it, he bestows a rogue charm about him which makes everyone accept him as he is. Apart from Raphael who still attempts to polish the rough diamond that he is, with meagre success. Personally, I picture a hard done Brad Pitt when I see Walter.

The entire conception of that character didn't take long, he seemed that he was already there all along with his black and white Great Dane, Bud, following him, stepping out of a French car from the nineties which he had tweaked like a new version of 'Kit', a bit marginal and mouthy who just stands for rights, and laws which promote everyone to use a heart.

His name de-constructed: Walter stands for altering the big W, changing the World for the better, so it becomes a peaceful lovey-dovey place, respectful of all within it.

Workmaster, not particularly because that human is hard work but because he is working the Angels hard, or whoever has some power in this world. He will be the forever questioning soul that demands that things are put to right. He is the one who fights fate and dares to dream. He brings hope to many doing so.

Walter Workmaster in quotes and passages, dive in with this down to earth dreamer:

'The being obliged and with great physical pain exhibited the bridge of its foot. It was marked by 666, forming a kind of pattern, with their tips touching. It was not a tattoo, it had been deeply stamped upon It, probably by a hot iron. He considered the mark dreading its implication, and muttered,

-Fuck it. I don't believe in any of that shit. If that caused your ordeal, human, you are in front of an unbeliever, therefore safe hands. Let's get you out, It.

He put the proposed code upon the lock: I-T-6-6-6. He smiled widely as a clicking noise announced the unlocking of the cage. He opened its door and presented his arms to It, helping the naked human out,

-Come here, poor thing, no more shit hole for you.

He realised that the being was a young woman, so damaged that she was unable to stand or walk. He carried her away within his strong arms, headed for the manhole and exited the bunker as fast as he could. His dog waiting for him, wagged its tail at his emergence. As he pulled the body of It before him, the dog turned around her, smelling her and pushed her with its nose to make her react somehow. The woman moved weakly, showing her face, trembling. The dog licked her pale visage, crying slightly doing so. He took the little human within his arms once more and told his dog,

-Yep, I know, she bloody needs a good clean, but I don't think that your tongue will do, Bud. I don't know how you are going to both fit in the car but we will figure it out.'
(verse 2: Code 666)

'Walter stood confronting the tall Doctor and shouted, tears coming to his eyes, pointing all the while to the skeletal woman,

-This is 'It', for Christ's sake: A fucking human being who had the bad luck, I am pretty sure of it to be born at the wrong time, wrong day, wrong month and wrong year. It was enough for others who thought it significant to mark her like a bloody beast and treat her like so. You want to know what the hell that is? It's a human in need, an appalling picture of what lack of reason can do and result of beliefs gone horrendously too far. Her state is similar to the one we saw in our history books of the victims of the holocaust. You want to know what is going on. Let me tell you, if you can't bloody see someone that needs your help any more just because it has a mark with some cultural or religious significance you are one of those 'good' self-assured 'convicted' of their convictions men who let horrors happen. Yes, the poor bloody thing was called It-666. My heart tells me an error was made somewhere; seeing a human treated like that, it tells me to help and do something. Obviously I made a mistake coming here. I always thought you had the soundest heart. I just heard horrors from it, Gabriel. Sorry to bring an injured and abused human into your clinic instead of Bambi or an arse.'

(verse 5: Stating It-666)

'As Asha opened the body bag, Walter and Caro were smiling at each other, all snuggled up and intertwined within it. Caroline whispered,

-This was exciting, being rolled up to the A&E.

Walter replied as he lifted himself up from the bag,

-Indeed, my cock is in plea for a relief. Raphael, you torturing me with the very proximity of my ex-wife will not do. I love your niece to bits and she drives me crazy because she is going to give me none of it later. What's up with the big talk with Gab? He is a wicked bastard slash Angel but a good one in a righteous sort of way.

Azryel Mortimer grinned widely and mentioned with a slight cough,

-And that would account to forgiveness being given from the injured party.'
(verse 26: Raphael's heavy Cavalry.)

Doctor Gabriel Purallee, Archangel Gabriel.

Gabriel plays a very important character in the saga. We meet him in the first book as incarnated Doctor Gabriel Purallee.

Strangely enough that ambivalent Angel is the one that all turns to for some sort of stability. His clinic and his house serve as a refuge, the safe haven where one can hide to stay alive.

Gabriel landed the tough job, appointed by his uncle Raphael, to become the Guardian Angel of Walter Workmaster. The undercover incarnated Angel went about it by befriending the law student which was dating his younger sister, Caroline. Although there were many things Gabriel disapproved about Walter, they also had a lot in common, and the two befriended in a big way. Taking holidays, doing road trips together, the unconventional Walter was a human most suited to be looked after by the aloof Angel Gabriel.

Gabriel felled in love during his job with the twin sister of Walter Workmaster, the free spirited Wendy. Despite the disapproval of his uncle Raphael, the younger incarnated Archangel went ahead and betrothed the human. Opening his own clinic, closer to the large woodland he inherited from his father, Gabriel sought to distance himself as much as he could from his overwhelming uncle, and his Army of Angels. His wake was easily followed by his younger sister Caroline, now a doctor in her own right who went to work for him at his clinic. Her fiancé Walter did not go along very well with Raphael, so she was kin to follow suit her brother and avoid the war of words that Wrath and Workmaster always seemed to have. The crew was completed by Wendy, who accepted Gabriel's offer of becoming his receptionist.

If Caroline turned out to be a happy young bride at the sides of Walter Workmaster, with a thriving little boy to show for it, Wendy became increasingly worried by the possessiveness and insane jealousy of Gabriel. When just smiling to male customers, just like she did with everyone as a receptionist, caused questioning, she put her betrothal to Gabriel on standstill and ask for a proper re-think.

She also stepped away from her job in order to distance herself from the suffocating distrusting environment that reigned by Gab. It was meant to be a month of rethinking. Yet Wendy went to work as a PA for politician Paul Peterson. She followed him on his campaign around the US and failed to come back. Peterson, worshipping and a servant of the devil, human sacrificed Wendy to him, like he did with many humans, ritually.

Let alone to say, we have a mourning Archangel, with a massive guilt trip on his hands in Gabriel. He devoted his entire attention to the brother of his betrothed and his young family. Bringing back Walter from his breaking down brink mattered to his grieving self deeply.

The character of Gabriel bestows a heavy heart. That taciturn Archangel has a long past where grievous mistakes have been made on his part which he never mentions. From incarnation to incarnation, he carries a weight in his heart which prevents him to be truly happy. Unlike the other Angels, belonging to the Army of Raphael, and considering his past credential, Gabriel has decided to not take part in fights nor battles. He always steps aside from the other Angels, very much the outcast. Despite any efforts of Raphael to keep Gabriel involved and within the boundaries of their Angelic society, it is tempered down by their personalities who clashes more often than not.

Archangel Gabriel has a pattern in all his incarnations to chose occupations which will allow him to be solitary, but devoted to the welfare of humans via medicine. Hermit, monk or Doctor, Gabriel has the mind of a genius which despite impressing others can disconcert. A trip to his lab will unsettle many to the extent that they think of Gabriel as a somewhat mad professor. Seeing bits of demon in his test tubes and jars, many Angels have the fear of becoming Gab's lab rat for his strange experiments.

The somewhat independent and darkly clever Archangel has his curiosity rather picked by the young Beast that Workmaster brings to his clinic. She becomes a subject that he is only too eager to analyse very thoroughly. Intrigued by her, he is also touched by her apparent gentleness and fears the usually impulsive reactions of the leader of all Angels, Raphael, when he will learn the existence of the Beast.

However his tentative to hide It from the knowledge of his uncle fails. Too soon for his taste he has the heavy cavalry of the elder Archangel at his doorsteps taking control of the situation.

His strong interest in the mysterious teenager, but also his care to the welfare of her Being, accompanied by his medical attention have an unsuspected result: the Beast falls in love with him big time.

Despite seeing his position more as a mentor and a guardian of It-666, he gradually develops strong reciprocal loving feelings for her. Their forming partnership, is cautioned by others who monitor it closely.

The loner's life of Gabriel turns to its head by the arrival of the Beast. He is suddenly surrounded by many he would usually rather shun and his house is invaded. His odd ways, idiosyncrasies, brilliant creations, mad yet genial plans and projects come to the scrutiny of the community of Angels, especially of its leader, who conceives a scheme to reintegrate the younger Archangel amongst them by taping into his enormous potential.

I wrote Gabriel as a relentlessly industrious character, house proud, a tad OCD, with a quick temper which comes to the surface like a volcanic eruption, yet which will recede to provide full forgiveness for treading on his peculiar larger than life toes (just an expression although very tall, Gab is no BigFoot). An incredibly generous and caring host, only he thinks more of your needs than your own self, preceding them with a humility and humbleness of character which makes him serve you in his own house almost like a king.

He would crave for a little bit of respect however doesn't think he deserves any. After what happened to Wendy, the same applies to love in his mind.

If his home is desperately pristine clean with no speck of dust in sight, his soul harbours cob webs at every corner, where Gabriel gets tangled with only a desperate wish to atone for his heavy past. However he hardly confides nor lets anyone go near his internal trouble. The Beast somehow feels his strong pain and has only the desire to palliate it, throwing her devoted self at his feet.

Although Gabriel is an intensely sad and stern character, a severe one: life is not to be taken as a joke or a fun fair ride, he bursts hilarious bubbles by his short temper properly scolding others. The other characters take bets to guess the reaction of Gab to their actions, did they provoke the short fuse in the usually gentle and caring Gabriel or not?

Almost sown onto his shoulders is the nickname of 'Killjoy', the one that thinks the World will end if he sees a drop of water not wiped up in his sink. Stepping a little too far of his particular line in his own house can potentially unleash Big Gab fetching his baseball bat to correct you a tad. Walter Workmaster had a memorable taste of his bat which did become a teasing banter between the two. If the bat broke the shoulder of the man, it did not break their strong bond and friendship. Beside Gab felt ever so sorry of that particular event, despite the human having pushed his boundaries.

Boundaries, this Archangel is full of them: if they were straightforward, it would be easy not to cross them however they are peculiar and complicated, as intricate as his massive hand built tree-house. Environmentally friendly, the craft that went into his home mesmerises whoever steps into it. Built from scratch from his own sheer laborious plans and work, the tree-house of Gabriel is any child's dream come true. His woods are the perfect place to hide a Beast, his home, her perfect nest, his heart a protective place for her to recover from any of her hardship.

Gabriel possess the strong welcoming heart which can harbour an hailing Beast. He knows the toll of hardships of the soul to and through to try to teach It to overcome them. This intimidating Archangel is a colossus with Achilles' heels, yet also with all encompassing wings. He is the Angel who tamed the Beast to be his Bambi, his nickname for her.

The choice of his surname, Purallee, was to symbolise what the character represent: the laws of the forest. That character full of principles not only lives in a tree-house in vast woodland, he is a marginal with self made laws.

Let's meet Gabriel in quotes and passages:

'Walter holding It-666's left hand reassuringly, pointed to her left foot and stated,

-I think for her ordeal, it has all to do with her mark, Gabriel, branded on her foot.

Purallee took a good look at the bridge of her foot and put it down immediately, as if he had burnt himself somehow seeing her triple six mark. He couldn't believe his eyes, thinking that his worst nightmare had finally taken human shape. He gave a bewildered look at Walter,

-Holy mother fucker, Walt! What did you fucking bring in my clinic? Shit, man, bloody hell! All of a sudden I prefer Bambi ran over by you, and plucking bullets from a man's arse! Holy crap, It was under a pentagram made with blood, has a heartbeat to sky-rocket you to the moon, and the bloody mark of the Beast on it. It's in my bloody damn clinic, you must be having a laugh, man! What the hell is that? What the hell is going on?'
(verse 5: Stating It-666)

'-Walt seems to think you had the bad luck to be born on the wrong day, is that so? What is your date of birth? Time and place if you do happen to know them too, please. I thought I told you to cease crying.

She bit her lip and wiped her tears with the palm of her left hand before picking the pen up to reply,

-Six of June ninety six. London. Six sixteen in the morning.

Gabriel grinned at the paper and raising one of his brows mocked,

-Are you scared of writing your date of birth in numbers, Beast? Don't you think it would cut the chase, making it simpler and faster?

It-666 closed her eyes taking the full blow of his remark. She could feel her other type of tears coming slowly but surely to her eyes. If she didn't want him to see how freaky she was, well this would not happen. She wrote down quickly,

-I am scared. I am a freak, I know I am. Sorry for these coming tears, don't be frightened, please don't.

She hid her face, lifting her arm to cover her eyes as much as she could, and the blood tears pouring now from them. Gabriel read her note, removed her arm from her face firmly yet with care, and lifted her chin to inspect them closely. He asked in a softer more concerned tone of voice, trying to tease and ease the mind of the Being in front of him,

-Well, well, what have we got here? Do you want to play peek a boo, Beast? I bet those hurt. Come, now, let's dry those. Do not be scared of me, I won't hurt you but I will examine you and assess you. I need to figure you out. Presently I have got to come to terms with seeing you being so sensitive, if I ever imagine an Antichrist you would not fit my bill. I am pretty damn sure you would rather want me calling you Bambi than Beast too, am I not right?

She managed to smile shyly as she agreed with him by a positive blink of her eyes. Gabriel pursued, as he collected a little blood of her tears upon a small tool and dipped the instrument into a test tube,

-Here we have it, finally a smile. I have to say that given all the shit that must have happened to you, I find you a rather gentle thing, polite and well behaved. Of course I am not going to give into it. So 1996, makes you sweet sixteen on human terms, a teenage Antichrist, but like Walter said some mistakes must have been made somewhere, for if I read my holy books correctly, I was rather expecting the opposite sex to yours. As I have my blood tear sample now let me wipe the rest, and try to be less emotional Bambi.'
(verse 6: Dark Angel Gabriel)

'Now, let me ask, Bambi, what went on with the Bud thing? This was a tad unsettling. Can you explain this to us?

It-666 clutched tightly Gabriel's hand as she confessed, her eyes pleading for his comprehension,

-I do something to animals. I don't know what. They always come to me, are extremely well behaved and friendly to me but they also become overprotective of me. However, I talk to them directly or their minds and they obey. Maybe it is because I am truly a beast, and we speak the same language.

Gabriel welcomed her confession, stating,

-This skill doesn't make you a beast for some humans were bestowed with this peculiar gift, the most famous of all, King Solomon.

Walter went to one of the windows, opening it wide, and told full of circumspection,

-Right, saying 'Down' to my dog and him executing the order doesn't ring Solomon's mythical skill to me. Impress me, Bambi, call the little birds in here, and as you will fail, it will prevent Gab, going all biblical on us!

Doctor Purallee shook his head in disapproval, and ordered,

-Close that damn window, you, Muppet! I don't want any fucking birds shitting in my clinic.

Birds, large and small came flocking in, yet all perched upon the window sill, with some singing melodiously. Caroline clapped her hands like a child at the sight of the little robin, blue tit, wood pigeon, blackbird and collared dove mix. She expressed her emotions with a bright smile,

-Looks like Walt Disney's magic to me, Bambi!

Walter looked totally bemused, and nodding to the girl, he admitted,

-That's cutting my quack short! I am dumbfounded. You can let them go now, before one of them poops in his damn clinic, and before Gab gets his magical bat to show he is all out of patience with me!

Gabriel stood up with authority. All the birds went. He closed the window then ordered,

-Focus,children! Task at hand.' ...
(verse 14: Solomon's Power.)

Caroline Workmaster.

The ex-wife of Walter Workmaster is the human and younger sister of the incarnated Gabriel Purallee and the mother of the incarnated Michael. In Angelic terms, she is a very special person chosen to carry one or more Angels back to their incarnated form. Did she knew about it? She had no clue at all. She had no conception that her son, brother and uncle are Archangels until she stumbles upon an Angelic meeting led by Raphael at his AA club in the middle of the night. Like her husband, humans have no ideas that Angels are walking among them and looking after them and Earth. It is a secret which is revealed to her as her uncle facing the hard choice of either erasing the memory of her niece or letting that human know about the presence of Angels in the world, chose the latter risk. Brain washing Caroline is out of the question for him, purely and simply because the Archangel has a soft spot for the human he helped raising but he also has respect for her original individuality, which reminds him of his own self.

When the human parents of Gabriel and Caroline passed away in a car crash, Raphael took them on. Gabriel was fourteen while Caro was just under ten. If the little girl hardly spoke of her childhood, or parents, Gabriel mourns in complete silence in his bedroom for days on end. Their uncle reacted to their loss by providing for them to the brim. He spoilt them. With an army of bodyguards newly appointed nannies to attend to his niece and nephew, Raphael lavished on them. One reason was that the Archangel did not allow himself to have children of his own. More than a niece, he considers Caroline has a daughter, a human he loves watching over or after from afar or close.

Spoilt brat Caroline in his home, took an unusual turn for the better or the worst. She resented having been decorated like a doll by her mother, been put on a mantle piece with the order to stay put and pretty. Caroline, in Raphael's large clubs, apartments where one can get lost, breaths again. She is rapidly her boisterous self which escapes her appointed 'nannies' with an alarming regularity to just enjoy herself. The rejection of her early years, as a child totally dependant on others will, which wanted her to only sit pretty and silent, had all her wishes being fulfilled in Raphael's guardianship. He freed her personality and let her express herself. She went all tomboy at his at first, wearing dungarees and shirts, with her hair cut short. It then developed into a daring do teenage-hood which Raphael remembers with some fondness: Expect the unexpected and you will have a Caroline standing at the end of it.

Watching over a very human Caroline was like watching over the world for the Archangel, he didn't know where it will end, where he will have to pick her up next, from a drunken spree in Glastonbury or a police station for taking part in an illegal race car rally with no licence whatsoever and winning it.

Only Gabriel bestowed that calming influence on his sister, only he was daring enough to tell her right off. The growing Gabriel saw Caroline as being too indulged like a danger will happen to her. His good old advice did not blame her for one bit, he just encourage her to make something of herself. He understood the big display she made during her teenage years and where it came from. He channelled her energies to help her concentrate on being her true self, not the negative of someone else wishes upon her. He managed to get her to some sort of studying mode making sure she would go to university.

Wild Caroline met Walter Workmaster at university. He was a charismatic law student who led the others and challenged the old establishment wherever it failed to address current issues. She had had a string of boyfriends prior to him but none quite met what she was after and she split with them very rapidly. She never presented anyone to her fearsome uncle, although he was aware of every single one of them because of his appointed nanny/bodyguards following Caro everywhere. However by then, Caroline, disliking too much scrutiny which prevented the potential for her to be naughty, had developed to an art form ways of escaping their attention and escaping. When his niece finally presented him one of her conquests, Raphael just knew that Caroline was very serious with that particular one. Despite disliking Walter Workmaster who was not afraid to contradict him on any point at first sight, Raphael could only admit that the young man, however humble his backgrounds were, had a positive influence on his niece. Not only was she following the student in his fight for human rights wherever it took him, she was following his advice on many thing such as stopping using recreational drug.

Experimental Caroline cleaned up her act overnight for the blue eyes of Workmaster. He was her perfect match, the man that could captivate her attention for hours on end without boring the life out of her. With Walter she didn't know what to expect: taking a train to protest by the white house or revising for her exams while he wrote articles fighting for human rights over a picnic sitting on the grass. If her uncle didn't seem too keen on Walter, all too serious Gabriel befriended the young man. She had no idea that her brother was in fact appointed by her very Archangelic uncle to do so.

Caroline is a bright and vivacious character. She has energy in abundance. Like Walter, she is headstrong and it is hard to stop her if she has decided to fight for something. No one could stop her marrying Workmaster, even if his fortune did not match hers.

The marriage to Walter was an happy one. However her bubble burst dramatically when she saw him break down in front of her eyes. The horrendous death of Wendy devastated the man to a point close to insanity. Caroline felt totally out of her depth and unable to control the situation. Reaching out to Walter was impossible and she saw him almost slipping away from her life as he tried to take his. The prompt intervention of Gabriel rescued the man. But it was a breaking point for the young couple.

Caroline took the tough decision to split from Walter in order to protect her son from seeing his father like that. This made the matter worst rather than better. But the upset Caro is a character that will take clear cut choices without thinking of the consequences or the hurt she may cause. She will engage in a large scale tit for tat. If Workmaster did not consider her and her son in his grief and intention to kill himself, she will hold that grudge against him and just walk off instead of being comprehensive. For her offended, saddened and frightened self, her heart could have screamed to her husband: how dare you wanting to leave us like that. You are ready to depart, me too, watch me and my son walk out of this door.

However Caroline is a character far from proud to have taken that bold step away from broken down Walter. She is laden with regrets. Despite having stepped aside, she keeps tabs upon the welfare of Workmaster. She is desperately worried for him and gets involved with his recovery by making sure the man understands that he will always be able to see his son and keep in contact with him.

At the start of the saga we meet a couple with a past. They are separated but put them in a room together and they have that affection for each other that just transpires from them in millions of subtle ways. Caroline would probably indulge in teasing the downtrodden Walter, but she will also be protective of him verbally.

Caroline has put a stamp on that man for the better or the worse: he maybe an 'arsehole' sometimes (the other nickname she has for her Blondie Bear) but he is 'her arsehole', the only one allowed to get on her tits in a big way. Forgive my language, this is to give you the feel of plain and straight talking Caro, tomboy at heart that will not take any shit lightly.

I have not many female characters in this saga, however whenever you meet one she will be fighting her own corner. The birth of Caroline in my head was like having a hand full of cards, with the difficult choice to do to chose which one would I lay on the table that can match or just meet Walter Workmaster on a certain level. In the game of cards theme, 'Caro' is 'carreau' in French: the diamond. She is Walter's queen of hearts and the treasure of her uncle. Her first name is influenced by MC Solar's song 'Caroline'. I had to create my Caroline.

She is a tough cookie girl that can take a right bite and make you crumble. As for visualisation she parades in my mind as a look a like Halle Berry with short hair. No wonder Walter fell for her, she is a stunner.

Let's meet Caro in quotes:

'-Caro, it's me.

The exasperated voice stated,

-I know it's you, Walter, there's only one arsehole that can possibly wake me up in the middle of the night! Twelve fifteen, are you drunk out of your mind again?

His lips grinned slightly as he tried to smooth the temper of his ex-wife,

-Caroline, it's an emergency. I need you at your clinic Asap.

The voice snapped,

-Go to the ER! I haven't the Au-pair girl tonight. I can't leave Micky on his own. As you are still talking, I am sure you will survive.

-It's not for me, Caro. Hunting trip gone bad. ER is a no go. DIY job required, non-disclosure. Take Micky with you.

-I will be there in half an hour. What can I expect?

Walter smiled knowingly, the caring Caroline was now on the line, listening attentively. Somehow he knew he could always count on her.'
(verse 3: Calling Earth.)

'Caroline pushed her plate in front of her, and looked in desperation at the three men. Then, with almost begging eyes, she pleaded her case directly to Azryel Mortimer, and Raphael,

-I only said the truth as I lived it at my door. You can't frighten people the way that you do without consequences. I am a weak fucking woman and I fucking fainted. And if I had my normal day, my normal night, a smaller shift, less adrenaline, fear and anxiety, a little more food earlier, I would have been my stronger self who would have shown you my two fingers in a rude fashion.

Correct me if you will for being honest but what would be the purpose? Teaching me to lie, and be nice when I feel that I am being stepped on, and trampled upon regardless of any feelings I may harbour. You can't possibly put the constant threat of torture upon my mind, and expect me to say great, I am very happy about that my dear uncle, let's get on with it! You must be joking. That's wrong! Honestly, how do you want me not to speak my mind about it at some point?'
(verse 22: Eat It All.)

'Caroline pulled her legs back against her, feeling a little insecure, and swore,

-Blimey! I wish I was not so asthmatic right now, I would ask for a cigarillo and join you in a seen it all, cynical smoke. I am speaking to Death at what, four in the morning, about Angels, Archangels, demons and carriers. Let alone seeing an Antichrist yesterday, at about the same time, and I can only swear like my Walt, in his usual way, 'that's a fucked up bloody mess, baby, but don't worry, we will work it out, eventually.'
(verse 23: The Angelic Anonymous Apostasy.)

Michael Workmaster.

We meet Michael, age eight, called Micky by all. This important Archangel has only recently incarnated once more and his human childhood makes him be temporally at a vulnerable stage. However he was given parents of choice in Walter and Caroline. Both are nurturing and loving him to bits.

Like the Beast, this character is at an early stage at the start of the saga. Unlike her, he was provided with a loving childhood, which makes him a very happy, bouncy kid Being. He has bags of tenderness for everyone which he wears on his sleeve. From his currant human parents, he gathers that loving understanding and open minded acceptance. Faced with a brand new member of the family, called the Beast, and not being an only child anymore, he just takes her hand and shows her what it is to enjoy a bit of childhood. His heart adopts It-666 almost like his father, without question.

Micky is a character who rallies others and unites them by his mere presence or absence. His abduction brings about the strong coalition between the Beast and Raphael's Angels. They fight together for the first time to retrieve him at all cost.

We know Michael is special but we do not know exactly how at the start of the saga, just like we do not know how the dysfunctional human Walter Workmaster is. They are crucial individuals which are worth saving for they bestow the future of all in their hands. They create unity, spread love like if it was golden butter on any dry heart, filling every hole of the bread with melting goodness. The worst thing they can possibly cause is an heart attack, imposing a rethink on how we deal with others because of politic or religious views. Both characters stand firmly against religious and ethnic cleansing, pure genocide. If his human father constantly voice and plead for love, Michael will fight to establish it once and for all.

Michael is an apocalyptic Archangel who will cull the Beast if it comes to it, however she was found at an early stage of formation, and all have a given chance to turn their fate around, and be really human with a sound heart not a murderous one. It-666 listens and responds to the human love of the Workmasters who accepted her in their split apart family, which works well nonetheless, as a loving unit. They are teaching her to love humanity and Michael will give them a hand doing so. If it is the last call, the last chance, he will be there doing it like his human father. Both are making 'It', giving her hope for a better future where she has a fair chance in it like anyone else. Their hearts are loving and all inclusive and the teenage Beast can recover by them. She develops a strong loyalty to them.

What else can I say about Micky? He is a character to watch.

Writing his character has been a little difficult for I know who he becomes in the future. From A to Z, where do you go? His path has similarity to the one of the Beast in an opposite kind of fashion.

However I can answer one question with a straightforward response, Michael is a lovable character, one that makes you hope for a better future like his human father. I was very much inspired by 'little lord Fauntleroy' character nearly all my life, and little Micky is a response to it. However the cute sweetness of the character is mixed by the big future the young Archangel has ahead of him as a warrior.

In physical incarnated shape, the human Archangel, with a white father and a coloured mother, is an awesome lovely mix: He is love and what love is made of.

Raphael Wrath, Archangel Raphael, aka Wrath.

Wrath is a character which tells you how it is in his standards and will force you to them by any mean, without almost any regards for who you are. Raphael has a physical presence that can make you quiver and he knows it. He plays with it shamelessly like a cat on a mouse chase. He can make it as sweet or cruel for you depending on his plans, schemes and temper. Wrath is renown to have a very short temper, trying him is definitely a bad idea. He comes with strings attached. He is full of them. Worse, he is the leader of them: anyone he pulls can spell your doom or your blessing momentarily. Raphael as a puppet master could be all good if his mind would not switch in a nanosecond to an entire other direction. Raphael is frighteningly so impulsive yet it is also his main skill, quick thinking, acting fast, he kills anything in the bud before it can fester away.

In the first book of the saga, we encounter Raphael Wrath still in his human incarnated heyday. Wrath is full of himself, ready to blow away anyone out of his path yet he is asked to consider who could be his worst enemy's life. His fiery reaction is to impose a meeting with the Beast. However their encounter leads to their fighting together partnership more than anything else. The Archangelic leader can count on a new recruit in his army with specific needs he has to cater for. He has the angelic force to do so and the right angel for any task. Beside he can turn a Beast into an Angel anytime, just let him introduce her to his missions and fights upon earth.

Raphael Wrath throughout the saga is a handful of a character. Leader of the pack, he directs all to follow his way, right or wrong, if it turns wrong, he will direct it back to the right direction. He is questioned throughout by Walter and his dreaded sidekick, Azryel, the Angel of Death, who is serving as his henchman.

Big time mobster of an Angel, loaded to the brim with a questionable wealth, he is the one who took the lead of the Angelic Army with credentials proved by his missions and battles. Highly regarded, he rules over the Beings in the world. His decisions are followed to the letter like his orders.

Raphael is that unashamed controversial individual that would lead a crowd to their freedom. He does express his wrath rightly. A warrior, he has survived many fights, he is there to stay, whatever happens: he has a fair chance for he has put his hands and meddled with everything. Playing poker, he will always have a winning hand. You can bet safely on his side. You might just stay alive for another day or eternity.

Like a double edge sword, his decisions can bring a battle to a winning end but also to a lot of blood. He is an incarnated Archangel who can spell it for you backward and forward if you ask him to. In that I mean that he has the scope to take drastic actions. When none would do so, Wrath will bring justice down to earth, and use whatever way to achieve it.

Wrath's ways are not for the faint hearted however they preserve humanity by protecting it.

His character demands a lot of the other characters especially prompt exactitude. He doesn't suffer fools lightly nor does he tolerate any trying to fool him. His exigence are truth and honesty for all who wants to be in his society. He watches over a large society which encompasses the safety of other incarnated Beings that walk the Earth in secrecy and also making sure that they respect humans. If they do not, he applies his laws and intervenes to rectify the situation. Punishment for misconduct may be handed to be delivered by his right arm, Azryel, then the result on the guilty party might end in a lethal way. But if he applies it, himself, as he is also one of the established Punishers upon Earth, the consequences might still be costly for a life or many, as he has a hot headed tendency to be heavy handed. His nickname given by all, 'Wrath', means it all, but as his surname it is implying that he represents the Wrath of God.

On the other hand, almost like a king, he will reward, lavishly, loyalty and good hard work. Raphael takes pride in his Army and his soldiers. Where he lives, they will live. That may means his large labyrinth like penthouse flats he has in his various properties all over the world, or sleeping rough with his men on any ground, on any mission. This character, who is quick to express his displeasure, sometimes physically, has difficulties to express how satisfied he is with anyone in words, so he will do so in gestures, more often than not in a materialistic way. He also expresses his loving care to someone that way. When he spoils one, it indicates not only the recognition he has for that individual but also the affection he has for them.

Speaking of affection, Raphael is a family man without a direct family of his own. Patriarch, godfather, he will look after you in ways sometimes totally unnoticed or unknown. He will never be ashame to pull strings to protect who he calls his own, from humans, Beings or Angels. Provider and protector, if one of his run at his doorsteps, he or she will find him, maybe frighteningly interrogating, yet, afterwards ready to respond to the request in a most informed, appropriate manner. He may not disclose to you how he will deal with it, but he will.

Think of a hammer that strikes a nail in, it symbolises a lot of Raphael's ways however the character, although leader of a group and imposing laws to the entire world, listens and does so carefully. He enquires, digs in the dirt, not afraid of what he will find out, or of what he will have to sort out. He rather knows about all the hurts and pains of everyone but also crimes for that gives him all his clues on how to bring a situation to a close.

Raphael can be seen as a harsh character. But if you put yourself into the warrior shoes of an Archangel that has been constantly relied upon to make the decisions and the toughest ones for an eternity, you will appreciate where he comes from better.

For the juicy bits, Wrath is a leonine character with the most charismatic gift to be extremely handsome. He knows it and plays upon it without shame. His unusual beauty draws people to him, and he is not afraid to use his beguiling charm to influence anyone to do his will or bidding. In any of his incarnated shape his physical strength and good look follows through with minute changes. At the start of the saga, we meet him age 76 looking like a thirty year old man. His fitness makes you wonder how that is possible for any human of that age. But he is an Angel given a human body for a while and he will stretch its limit to the maximum until he decides to switch to another one. This is a big task for Angels for they choose their human parents with a silently watching scrutiny for they will have to look after the most vulnerable part of the life of an incarnated Angel. Incarnation means a possible human death and losing their eternity for Angels yet Wrath and Azryel keep on top of things to prevent it happening to their soldiers.

When his vert-de gris eyes set on someone, that person has absolutely no choice but to be true to him and reveal any thing he knows to the Archangel. Wrath will find out the truth anyway and then the consequences will be a thousand times harsher than saying so in the first place.

Speaking of the look of a lion, Wrath bears a right mane of dreadlocks, salt and pepper, as long as his waist line. It is like his very independent signature mark: he dares to be awesomely different from the rest. He has also a mixed complexion which also speaks of sheer unity, a symbol of his strength and ability to deal with Beings, gods, demons, Angels and humans alike.

However Wrath is a controversial character, so abrasive that he can strain his relationship with others very easily. His dominant solar personality clashes regularly with the more reserved yet independent one of Gabriel.

Their misunderstandings of one another cause them to keep their distance but despite that Big Gab knows that he can count on Raphael to always run to his help. Wrath tries to repair their differences in odd ways, like making the younger Archangel incarnating in the mist of his family as his nephew. This still had mix success even when Raphael took charge of Gabriel and his sister at the death of their human parents. Wrath simply fails to understand the desire of Gabriel for complete solitude. It is alien to his own nature who enjoys being surrounded. Compounded to that Raphael fears that the younger Archangel sinks slowly but surely in a procrastinating loneliness where the heavy weight of his past mistakes would make Gabriel lose his wings rather than keeping them. Wrath can not accept seeing an Angel which he considers one of his becoming dangerously close to a complete fall. He will attempt in every way, back, left and centre to bring back, push back Gabriel in the mist of the other Angels who can provide his nephew moral support and a way of dealing with his issues. Somehow, out of nowhere, well actually a shit hole under a pentagram, comes the Beast, the young It, which will help him to do just that, preventing the fall of a major Archangel. Raphael watches the developing affection and devotion of It to his nephew with no aversion.

He is actually also kin to promote it. A big dollop of love might be the solution for Gabriel and a way to secure It, big time, on the Angelic side for all eternity. His matchmaking intentions and schemes are spotted by Walter Workmaster who has at first a certain aversion to them (for many reasons, Wendy's fate being one of them) however he warms to them and becomes irresistibly the accomplice of Wrath in the matter.

Strangely enough, Walter and Wrath have that love and hate relationship going on with each other. Their bickering is sometimes almost constant. But one thing the Archangel is unwilling to do is to impose silence on the impudent human. He may fantasise to strangle Walter in his dreams however in reality the man utterly entertains him by being one, the only one with his Death Angel, capable and daring enough to challenge him. This fact alone gives him a lot of consideration for Workmaster. Moreover Raphael listens attentively to the man's arguments, he ponders upon them and may also acts differently because of them. Throughout the saga, they become unlikely strongly united in an understanding friendship yet a very teasing one. Each others taunts are a delight to write, starting from their great divide of fortune, one being filthy rich while the other is always on the brink of straight poverty, to the one of being a successful leader of an Archangel compared to Wreck-Man, a human who has lost almost everything from wife to child passing by his job as a human rights lawyer, passing by the way they look with Raphael taking so much pride on his appearance to

Walt, that doesn't even start to care of his hunting tramp look. They are two characters worlds apart of each other but they have a few things in common, their strong love to put things right being one of them. Both have that urge and impulsion to act fast. What is cementing their coalition, strong friendship, is the welfare of the young Beast. Both feels the duty to make sure she is alright, given a future and a fair chance, and both share the dream that given that love always provides, all will escape a fateful apocalypse. It makes them allies and more than that. Wrath considered Walter Workmaster as 'his' human from the start when he stepped into his eternal life, offending him by having stolen the heart of 'his' surrogate daughter in his mind, his human niece.

If the character of Raphael has issues in showing his love with affectionate gesture or words, it doesn't mean that he is devoid of love. He demonstrates it differently than others by his generous protection.

The arrival of the Beast on the scene causes him right concerns in an apocalyptic point of view and for humanity's sake, but he is astute enough to accept that Walter Workmaster's way to deal with It-666 might be the right one and to give it a good go, himself. Beside It seems to respond well to the all encompassing loving acceptance of the human. He can lift his eyebrows with circumspection at the man adopting the Beast yet this also springs an all array of ideas, schemes and plans in his head, from trying the same method and acquiring an extremely powerful Being in his Angelic Army to keeping your enemy very close is a clever thing to do, passing by lets attempt to transform the Beast to an Angel.

Wrath put It to the test and missions, observes her, from afar or closely. He knows her real father, Eremiel, his arch-enemy, for having nearly lost his life at his hands, but for the extreme intervention of Azryel who saved him. It would be an easy thing for him to come over and annihilate the daughter of his enemy, one that is meant to be an evil conception. But meeting the Beast, asked to consider sparing her by Walter, the leader of the Archangel seizes the opportunity, the magnanimous one, the merciful one, the scheming one to give that chance to the Being in front of him.

Unlike Eremiel, she has something he likes and appreciates most of all, a deep down honesty. He gives the supervision of her Being to the one of his unforgiving but most trusted Angel, Death. Azryel can dispatch any rats swiftly without them squeaking or causing any mayhem in the big world house, they are looking after. The little Beast will need her honesty to stay alive by his Death Angel. Through the saga, It-666 wins her colours in Archangel Raphael's eyes. His appreciation of her grows, book after book. So much so that he is willing to take her Being within the heart of his own family, partly to protect her, partly to protect the world: a win-win situation on his doorstep.

As much as the youngster offers to him her loyalty, powers and bravery, he provides her with his fearless protection, and ultimate accolade: Angelic wings. If Walter is the adoptive father of the Beast, Wrath becomes her godfather giving her something she would never have been able to conceive or imagine in the downtrodden state where he meets her.

But with a good helping of his strong scoldings, he gets that lost Being back to some sort of soldiering shape which can only draw respect from all.

The love that Raphael represents maybe tough love but it is love nonetheless and gets somewhere.

For the trivia, writing about Wrath, although hard, sometimes I disagree with his character strongly like Walter can do, is like going onto a roller coaster ride: Highs and lows, frightening, memorable, awesome, dipping into the deep end and back again to the top of an about to break ocean's wave. Would I go through a rough ride again following his footsteps, missions and endless schemes? Hands up, shouting, screaming from the top of my voice, with a massive grin etched on my face, I would write again for that character: again and again, listening to 'Little Green Bag', George Baker Selection, and the rest of 'Reservoir Dogs's' soundtrack. Yes, one must admit that the creation of Wrath was influenced by a love for Tarantino's movies and especially that one.

Like Walter I hate him but love him all the same, and would miss all the fun that Wrath provides with all his endless battles to save the Earth or just the life of one single human.

Let's meet the character in quotes and passages:

'At the entrance of the alcove, she froze, taking in the view of Uncle Raphael, upon a large black leather cushion, in a lotus position, eyes closed, hands resting upon his knees with fingers lifted and folded in awkward ways. He looked so young, so healthy, so in tune with his body and spirit, and yet so frightening all at once, like a living human mystery. Who could believe the man was seventy-six years old, when he could stretch his body into unbelievably hard yoga postures, when his face showed hardly any wrinkles, when his full set of bright white teeth could give you his gloriously wicked smile at any time? Dressed in loose black linen trousers, and a burgundy red cotton T-shirt, with his feet bare, his toned muscles, his salt and pepper hair tidied in dread locks that reached his waist, and most of all his rare complexion, he was still very much a looker for any woman alive. His vert-de-gris eyes opened all of a sudden and he asked,

-Is it a dare to stare or stare to dare, that you are uncomfortably enjoying, my child? I will not have you making miles to remain boringly silent at my sight and sides. Speak.'
(verse 20: Uncle Raphael: Who's the Daddy?)

'Raphael tapped his fingers in an annoyed fashion upon the table, and told in a commanding tone,

-My dear child, it is well past your bedtime. Eat your pudding and no more talking. Then off to bed. I will not have you spreading the seeds of Workmaster's sedition at my table, in the presence of my most useful men.

Caroline gazed alternatively at Asha and Azryel. One was totally impassive while the other looked intensely and smiled kindly at her. She picked up her dessert spoon and dived it into the banana split ice cream. She shook her head and whispered as if for herself, but to her uncle,

-You do know how to make someone feel like a wayward child. I guess I am

definitely not fitting into our world anymore. Anyhow I feel like it. I went astray, and will remain so.

Raphael grinned and replied harshly,

-That is what you get for going with a Stray.'
(verse 22: Eat It All.)

'The Archangel Raphael nodded, a serious look upon his face as he demanded,

-Az, we do like being straightforward, open and honest upon our actions rather than crafty and subtle. Now which factors do we have to consider? You seemed to describe the challenge as one coin, with two different possible sides, changing our luck, and game. Somehow, head or tail, and what it could entail worries me deeply. You appear to have gathered enough information to envisage both aspects. Please, go through those in details.'
(verse 23: The Angelic Anonymous Apostasy)

'As soon as the ambulance doors were closed, the Death Angel opened the body bag under the worried gaze of Caroline and Raphael. He explained quickly,

-The man is in a coma. But he has been badly messed up with by Gabriel. Somehow Gabriel tried to imitate the Beast and her powers. He failed. The only given safety net he got was from the young Beast. I need all my skills to bring him back fully and healthy with us. Walt is in danger at the present.

Raphael put his hands upon the chest of Workmaster and told in tongue,

-Death, use me to annihilate any effects of them both upon him. Save my nephew, my so much nephew in law.

His eyes glowing of pure gold, Archangel Raphael was ready to channel all his strength in order to give a better chance to Walter Workmaster. The Death Angel grabbed his Archangelic hand and teased in tongue,

-Isn't that man so peacefully quiet and asleep right now? We should embrace a

minute of silence for the miracle it is... peace at last.

Raphael grinned knowingly but confided,

-I love his cacophony. It keeps me upon my lawful toes.

Azryel channelled the Archangelic power to recall Walter totally from his dangerous coma. A blue light surrounded the human for a few seconds before the eyes of the wondering and worried Caroline which held Bud. When the Death Angel had finished, he sat back with Raphael and told reassuringly,

-Workmaster will come around now. Give him a few minutes. He will be okay.

When Walter stirred and finally opened his eyes, Raphael's concerned look vanished to be replaced by a wicked smile as he could not help welcoming the man,

-Here he comes, Trouble is awake.'
(verse 25: COMA, just a stroke not a Final Point.)

'As soon as the ambulance pulled in the car park of Dr Purallee's Clinic, Azryel was on the lookout for his men and sent them the telepathic order to show themselves. Ten black suited incarnated Angels stepped out from waiting cars and approached the emergency entrance where the ambulance stopped.

Asha opened the back of the ambulance, Azryel and Raphael pulled the trolley out carrying the large body bag and rushed into the emergency room, followed by the ten henchmen.

There Gabriel Purallee welcomed them. The tall Doctor gave an unfathomable look to Raphael before presenting him his hand to shake. Raphael refused the hand, his eyes incandescent and told,

-Honesty is what I ask from everyone. Asking for my help and lying about the subject puts you in the worst of terms with myself and my heavy cavalry right now. Not only that, the human in you care has been messed up badly by 'your' intervention. Death and I had to intervene to not make his one untimely.

Workmaster is mine as much as yours, I will not tolerate him and his health being played with by incompetent hands. The powers of the Beast and Death were not given to all for good reasons. Do not play the apprentice sorcerer, Gabriel and raise without order. The Powers will destroy you before you know it. And I would be given the supervision of the task. All my given tasks come to completion. Did I make myself clear, soldier?'
(verse 26: Raphael's heavy Cavalry.)

'The Archangel Raphael smiled with a little cruelty to the man stating,

-Do you want your son back safe and sound Walter, or in little pieces? Your quote Super Being, our young Antichrist has found the perfect Puppet Master in the Death Angel. She fears being used for Evil, We will use her for Justice and Good. If she strays with Us, we acknowledged her want and desire for death and we will grant it.'
(verse 28: About embracing Death. TrUsT.)

Azryel Mortimer, the Angel of Death.

If Wrath was daunting enough, his henchman is even more unsettling. What can I say to bring justice to Azryel's character? I absolutely adore writing him.

Azryel Mortimer is a character which grew a life from my pages and into my own heart. If there was a fan T shirt, black with a big red heart in the middle saying: 'I love Az', I would wear it proudly with no shame at all. It is odd for an author to say that they are the first 'groupie' of their created characters but I can only admit that I am for this one.

Azryel is the Death Angel, a born torturer, the ultimate Punisher of all worlds and all beings. Often coming unannounced into a room, he will observe you for a while before startling you. He enjoys that. His presence instills fear to anyone. Even Archangel Raphael hates being startled by his henchman's presence which he always fails to spot until the last minute. The fact that Azryel is the Ultimate Judge doesn't help the fear factor. Getting your acts right and together before him is a must. Being caught in the act by him is a terrifying prospect.

Servant of Wrath, Azryel Mortimer has a lot of duties, in fact he is always almost inundated by them. First and foremost, if Raphael is the leader of all Angels, Azryel is the general of the Angelic Army. His devotion to the Army and all of his soldiers is undeniable. He trains his soldiers in a harsh fashion and in the hope that they will never do a costly mistake on the battlefield. He abhors the thought of losing a soldier, even if it is just one. He doesn't want the death of a single one of them. Trainer and tough teacher, he has a strong protective instinct that will overwork his troupe until its soldiers know one move down to right perfection, so no one will falter and die in that dreaded eventuality. He is reverently feared by the Angels who are scared to disappoint, cross or worse fail him. Any making a mistake which if picked up by Azryel dreads the consequences of it, the punitive lesson that would inevitably come, teaching them the hard way to never do it again.

This is nothing yet compare to a poor criminal sod, demon or Being caught before their hour of death by the Death Angel. Depending on their life of crimes, the one to one, Death gives, is pure torture. In the saga there are a few instances when this occurs, is mentioned or we only see the result of it, if there is a result left to consider. No one dares asking Death to speak about the punishments he inflicted to the souls he had to deal with, apart for Wrath who as one Judge, himself, has the right to do so and can even step in during a punitive session. However it might not mean that he will make it stop, it can continue with the cooling control of his presence. Never forget that it is Archangel Raphael himself who gives the hard core criminals to Azryel to be dealt with.

The two Judges together have a frighteningly strong relationship. They have shared together many moments of almost an eternal history. The darker character out of the two, Death has many times saved Archangel Raphael, and one extreme instance, in order to do so, he used black magic which changed the eternal fate of all Angels in one stroke. For them to remain eternal, they had to incarnate in human shell again and again and again. However the fragility of their human shapes means that if killed within one it is a proper death with no returns. Whatever Azryel did that day, was followed by a terrible fight with fallen Archangel Eremiel. The atrociously wounded Wrath witnessed it all. It was a clash of the titans between Eremiel and Azryel, a fight where both would have ended dead but for a trick of Azryel which finished the fight. The fooled Eremiel left thinking his opponent dead. But the extremely damaged Death Angel went to Raphael, and processed to heal him as much as he could with whatever energy he had left to would let him do so. The saved Raphael, only witness of the fight, knew that Death partly damned himself during it and prior to it. He has seen what Azryel was capable of. If Eremiel was pure evil, Death could be a matching one. Bringing his Saviour back to his castle in the Kingdom of the Dead, the Archangel knew he was not allowed to tend to Death for he had condemned himself and his soul before his own eyes. Faced with Azryel asking him to cull him to prevent him to complete his damnation, in the fear that he would turned like another Eremiel, Wrath refused point blank. If Azryel wanted his own death, he could take it himself, if he wanted to retrieve the soul, he had been losing so fast within hours then, and only then, he would help him and give him a hand. The Death Angel sent him on his way, laughing at what he thought was pure insanity of a younger Judge than his experienced self: He was too far gone to be retrieved. However the leaving Archangel departed with his offer left open on the table, for consideration, and to come to him for a helping firm hand.

Three days past with the advent of Eremiel gathering forces among the Angels themselves, corrupting as many as he could, bringing fear to the rest. Now, not scared to be challenged, Eremiel was preparing to take control of everything. Archangel Raphael, losing hope on the situation, saw Azryel, still badly damaged, coming to him, and offering to him all he had and have left, kneeling and accepting the helping hand to retrieve the rest of his soul. From a King, Azryel became a servant, paying handsomely Wrath for the cost of the trouble of just attempting to gather back his soul.

The extremely feared Death Angel was a solitary Being or almost. He was imposed to train Raphael to be a Judge. Wrath was reluctant too to work with Azryel who he found far from pleasant, with a demeaning arrogance, silent or not. The put downs, he received at a mere mistake would have made him resent the character until he witnessed time and time again the way Azryel was collecting the souls of the innocents he had to pick up to take to his Kingdom, the ones who did not make it for one reason or another. He saw the tender side of Azryel, the heart of an Angel he always thought had absolutely none. From his training days, the Archangel grew respect for the older entity that Death was, slowly but surely. He came to realise that when Death took on particular hard cases from him, it was not to insult him as incompetent, it was to spare him from the toll it would cause on his shoulders. When Raphael was about to draw his last breath in the deadly trap from Eremiel, he saw an Angel in Azryel that cared beyond beliefs, ready to damn himself to save the life of another Angel. There was no way he would not try to help that Angel out of his damnation path. After all he owed his life to him.

From the moment, Azryel humbled himself in an extraordinary way to Wrath, (Death is the stronger one out of the two), their true partnership starts. It has complicity written all other it. Both know much much more than they let out, they are acquainted to the dark and the dirty, they appoint themselves the true opponents of evil. When none will come forward to fight it, the two will raise together as one to face it. They are demons diggers and fighters. They impose their laws across the world, giving a good hard run to Eremiel, to hide his evilness somewhere.

From his fight with Eremiel, Azryel learnt his techniques, his moves. Cunning, he kept the fight as long as he could to know all about his opponent. He offered that extreme knowledge to Raphael in the same time as asking him for his judging hand to kill him. He thought this would help Wrath's Army in their future fight. But as much as Azryel doesn't want to lose an Angel, and will do whatever it cost to save one, Raphael is the same. He refused Az's death wish. Whatever Wrath proposed brought him back an Angel who knew that his own death would bring the loss of the hard fought knowledge about Eremiel he had acquired confronting him to all Angels fighting evil. Wrath appointed Azryel as general and trainer of his Army, in the same time as taking him on as his servant.

Azryel is a larger than life character and he makes the hell of being a servant. Former King, knowing the entire scope of the powers he bestows in his entire body and else, with so much wealth of knowledge stored in his brain cells that it hurts them, he is to say the least very hard to deal with. Yet Wrath and him are like an old couple that will bare the other and bring the house on fire doing so. However they are completely devoted to one another. One would give his life for the other.

Throughout the saga, their exchanges go very deep as both have an extreme reliance on the other. They sound just like an old couple who had settled for one another for lack of choice, but come battles or just one facing a hard time and you will see the other right there, surrounding their alter ego with their entire support. I just love their strong seen it all eternal bond. It is a fighter's one born and bred in the battles they fought side by side. Az and Wrath are

Angelic blood brothers.

Together they make a fearsome unity against evil. Both well seasoned warriors and tough Angels, at the start of the saga, that will not take crap from anyone, especially from a 'spawn' of evil Eremiel. The young Beast has literally no chance at all. If Walter offers her the chance of a future, Wrath and Az put a clear condition to it: be good or be dead.

However the young It they encounter, that suicidal Being that does not know any better, compels them to take her on board, in the mist of their Army, where they can watch her closer. Given the task of the close monitoring of the Beast, her 'babysitting' or rather teenage-sitting: Azryel is reluctant and more than fuming. He'd rather be with his soldiers doing battles.

However meeting her, training her, he finds a Being with similar powers to his, with similar struggles. He can offer her his eternal experience for her to cope with her feelings of being just a monster. He can offer her the same hand that Wrath gave him, the one that tells you to grab it: that he will pull you through and you will never be the monster you are fearing to be.

If training the Beast to be a soldier grabbed all his attention, babysitting her as she is raised by Walt and Gab, brings his entire involvement. He becomes her confident, her best friend. Watching that young Being grow and fight by him, brings him more pleasure than his entire life can count. She makes his fighting day much better for she is a right warrior after being trained and when she set herself to not be her pacific self.

The discovery of the Beast was a true event for him. Here, he is, a dutiful Being asked to do the worst job in the universes, which he would not give to anyone else for their sakes for he know the toll it takes on one's soul, the Ultimate Punisher, a lawful killer. He meets a younger Being, which has the tender guts, suicidal ones, yet the courage to say no to her own life if her life means hurting all and an end to humanity. He understands the plight of It-666 more than anyone else. Even more so the Beast wears her heart on her sleeve.

She is honest to him like he had never seen anyone else do so before to that extent. She knows she can get killed by the result of any of her confessions, yet she does them. He becomes a mentor to that Being, giving his all to the mission of Wrath and Walt's dream of adverting the apocalypse.

Azryel is very far from being a born babysitter as you can very well imagine. His interactions with It-666 are ones to watch, sometimes deeply amusing, sometimes deeply heart warming, sometimes deeply distressing, as he gets to pick up her soldiering self back from many horrendous situations.

Like Walter, he will give to the Beast her very physical last chance to her last minute. If there is one Angel that can control It-666 if something goes wrong, it is him, and the good hearted Being lets herself be, live because of that. She lays her trust on the Angels, especially on Azryel: he will never let her go wrong. This is the only condition that makes her accept a future and a life. It is a win-win: Angels and It have a clear cut understanding.

The fact that she is the offspring of Eremiel doesn't stand the claim that the human Workmaster takes on adopting the lost It. All Angels will fight for that claim, right or wrong with their own lives for it offers hope for all, especially humanity.

Azryel had the closest encounters with Eremiel, like Wrath. They should hate all of his children yet they know better than hate for they are Angels. Taking on It gives them a right journey of the heart. All characters learn to love like it is their last day because of It. All are making up with one another, some are letting themselves love for the first time...

The Angel of Death takes on that incredible journey of the heart, and it is moving to see it book after book, one step at a time, from befriending to allowing himself to properly love.

In the first book of the saga, we meet Azryel Mortimer, the most terrible henchman there is to meet. He is a walking plight of a Being himself that gets to take all others away at some point dutifully. It is a burden which he loves to hate but also hates to love...

The character is atrociously interesting, with depth which goes down to deep darkness and brings you back up to the surface for a breath, which you hope with all your guts is not the last because you are enjoying it. I loved writing every minute of Azryel from his bespoke bling-bling: the cigarillos, the immaculate brown Richelieu shoes, the silver zippo and flask marked with his angelic symbol; to all his heartfelt sarcasms.

Death is caustic and sarcastic all the way through, he would pick a nit from your hair that you didn't know was there and destroy it with his fingers and words, bringing utter shame on you. However Azryel is a absolutely dark character, if he will prevent you to walk his path with all his might for you to remain good, he will go his way and disappear, come back eventually and you will not know where he went. The fact that he is back to help you should be good enough for you, like it is for Archangel Raphael.

It is a regular complaint of Wrath not knowing where his Death Angel has disappeared: 'Where's my Az?'. For one thing, it expresses his reliance on Azryel from his advice, pertinent comments to the bodyguard aspect of the Angel. After all Azryel is the only one that stands a chance to defeat Eremiel single handedly. More often than not Death would have been dealing with his deadly duty or a meeting with his Army of Soul-Takers. Those briefings deal and speak about the newly departed souls, usually they are full of heartbreaking sadness. Coming out of them, a deeply affected Azryel would stroll for a while, only coming back to the full of life Wrath when he is ready to face plain fight again. There's no time to mop by the Archangel. This suits the Death Angel.

For Azryel has a thrill seeking nature. The constantly scheming Wrath launches mission after mission, adventures after adventures with a bountiful energy. Being his sidekick allows Azryel to make sure Raphael doesn't burn his wings and stays alive but also gives him an eternal life far from boring.

That character loves what pick his curiosity, the unusual. He has lived for so long, that he enjoys when something sparks out of the blue which shows him that he has not seen it all yet. He loves watching and speaking to individuals who differ from the norm. The Beast fit his thrill bill with all her powers and her use of them. As for the annoying Wreck-Man Walt, Azryel relishes on his constant challenges and retorts, so much so that he likes the society of the human but also taunting him shamelessly. If they do argue the man and the Angel establish a strong friendship. In the second book of the saga there is an amusing scene where both are watching the 'Exorcist' and showing it to the Beast asking her to replicate some tricks, only to be stepped upon by a furiously scolding Gabriel. Az will have no remorse in calling the Archangel the Great Killjoy.

He has that wicked twist in his character that will make him thirsty for a thrill and grab it when the opportunity occurs. It can range from taking the piss out of someone shamelessly or going for a kill (there must be one demon to hunt lurking in the dark which he has not been found yet). He taunts because he can: A. He can take on anybody if anything turns into a fight, which he knows he will win. B. It gives him great enjoyment for a minute or more. None escapes from his constant sarcasms or teases, not even Wrath, who has more of his respect than anyone. At least when he plays fights with Raphael, he will fake losing to boost the confidence of the Archangel. This, he will never admit to, to protect the pride of Wrath.

Despite his wickedness, Azryel possess that tremendous care for others. Partly damned, he will give up the will of killing himself to make sure he teaches to others how to fight evil properly. Az take 'Care' as a duty of his heart. He doesn't know any better.

As a character, Azryel does have an exceptional sensitivity, sometimes hidden, sometimes not, every single act means to him, even the tiniest one. Hated by everyone, feared, the helping hand proposed by the younger Judge he trained is unexpected. Surely all should wish him dead and dusted. The fact that one doesn't, is enough for him to carry on, and devote his entire fighting loyalty to him. A simple offer of friendship by a human touches him deep down. He is that terrifying Being that is rarely the recipient of a little care, friendship or love, so when he receives some, like a wild stray, he will bark at who dared to stroke his rough fur, but hours later he will come back to that person, lick their hand and offer to be their protective guard dog, his most dutiful care.

Talking about Azryel would not be complete if I did not touch upon a human that was bold enough to declare her love to the Death Angel: Liz Arczy. Without knowing it, the red head turned his eternal life upside down.

Returning to the dog analogy, just a tad, like the Beast likes nature and animals so does Azryel. For him it has to do that he prefers their company more than the one of Angels or humans. They are more likely to be purely innocent compared to the others. As a little Angel going to his deadly meeting with his Soul-Takers in the deep darkness of the forest, he was accompanied by a pack of wolves, licking his frozen fingers warm. When no humans nor Angels would get close to him, animals did. Even if the Death Angel would say casually that if he had any spare time, he would take on a hobby like other people do, then mentioning in a questionable list 'butchery' as one he contemplates, even if we do not know if he is in earnest or just teasing, give that Angel a dog or a puppy and see what happens. Having to look after the Great Dane of Walter Workmaster, Bud, just for a few hours pleases Death more than he can say. Animals soothe him, looking after them, seeing them, walking with them. The observant Wrath picks up on that, and like with everyone he will try to work out ways to keep any coping happily with their lot by bestowing upon them a bespoke gift...

Like Wrath, Azryel is a childless Angel, even more so for he has not got any relation at all, nor nephew or nieces to lavish upon. Instead his devotion to Raphael makes him regards the Archangel's family, a tad like his own. Although both can be highly critical of Gabriel, Walter and Caroline, they love them from the bottom of their hearts. They would protect them with teeth and claws if needs be. Concerning little Micky, or It for that matter, Az is absolutely fond of the younger generation of Workmaster's. He enjoys child sitting their Being's youth. A trip to a pet shop to let them chose respective pet hamsters makes his day, takes him away from the dead and dread back to the world of the living. It's a pure simple pleasure.

For the trivia, I was inspired by Samuel L Jackson as 'Jules' in Pulp Fiction while writing about Azryel, however the character blended to the near physicality of the singer 'Maxi Jazz' in my mind whenever I saw him. (especially in Faithless's track video: Insomnia). 'Insomnia' would be the desperate tune of Azryel Mortimer, his favourite one, for he can not get sleep either.

Always awake, always fighting, always walking from one problem to another, with for only respite his well earned smoking breaks, Azryel fares through his eternity. Blame him if you will for his casual smoke or sip, or take his job instead, although he will never let you do so, fobbing you off quickly from his dispatching patch before you can get hurt like him.

Let's meet him, do not be afraid, he is the Ultimate Soul Taker, one with an Army of Angels, but also one with an Army of Soul-Takers... Just make sure your heart is good when you meet him, just make sure you respected god's first commandment and did not kill anyone, otherwise you will meet a thousand virgin flames licking you, red and raw.

Quotes & passages:

'Raphael pointed to his unconscious niece and almost shouted, full of growing wrath towards the unknown new powerful player who dared to warn him, Archangel Raphael. What was the warning about? He will have to find out and the answer was with Gabriel, he was sure of it.

-Kind! Do you call that kind?

Azryel shrugged his shoulders and held Caroline's hand within his. His long fingers glowed with sparks of blue electricity that he sent to her body waking her up doing so, slowly but surely, he replied,

-I call that kind. Instead of Sleeping Beauty, Raphael, you could have a

cadaver, right now upon your sofa. It has the power to kill all yet it doesn't. I have the same power, and I unkindly obey my orders, without exceptions, all in 'good' time...'
(verse 21: Tell me all about It?)

'She saw Raphael trying to order the Great Dane of Walter about to no avail. When ordered to sit the dog would lay on the ground, and if laid upon the ground already he would stand up right away. Azryel Mortimer, seated upon the leather cream sofa nonchalantly, couldn't contain his ironical laugh at Raphael's fruitless attempts. However as soon as he spotted Caroline, his smile disappeared, his face becoming deadly serious, he stood up politely and warned Raphael of her presence within the room.

Her uncle turned to her with a sigh full of desperation,

-Walter's dog is a beautiful one, but also the most useless and stupid, I must say. How long will I have to look after it? It needs complete retraining! But I can afford it.

The Great Dane rushed to Caroline, wagging his tail to her. She put her hand upon his head and made him follow her without any struggle. As she stood before her uncle, she corrected him by a simple demonstration. As she snapped her fingers together, the dog sat by her, in an almost statuesque position, and explained,

-The dog is fully trained. But Bud was trained by Walter. Which means he will only answer to him, as the traditional orders do no apply to him in the usual fashion. You have a month to work those out uncle Raphael, but I would be very disappointed if a spell in your dominion means that our Bud becomes an ordinary dog.

Azryel asked all of a sudden, kneeling by the dog, his wicked smile back upon his face,

-Frustrating Workmaster, as always! Which training method did he employ?

Caroline answered him, worried by his picked interest,

-Purely and simply Pavlovian.

Azryel tried a few words, falsely at random, watching carefully the effects upon the Great Dane, and stated

-Classical conditioning, Raphael. Good old Walter just messed up with the words and substituted the real orders he wants by gestures. If you let me keep that dog overnight, I will know his control pattern and reflexes and we will know how to order him about the Workmaster's way. I would not spoil his amusing frustrating work upon his dog, I respect it. I haven't laugh as much since a while.

Raphael looked at Caroline with desperation, commenting,

-Right, your Walter, even not present has managed to make me look like a fool in my own home for a good half an hour. You couldn't marry someone normal, could you? Azryel, as long as you understand twisted in human behaviours and animals one, I will gladly let you in charge of that bloody dog. By the way, I do like that breed, and if you do fancy training unusual guard dogs that look the part, Azryel, I would welcome about five to eight puppies of those, either blue, grey or glistening black.

Azryel stood up raising his eyebrows deeply amused,

-Yeah, right, half an hour of Raphael with a damn dog and I end up with the tall order of eight puppies to raise into guard dogs. I put that into the account of the Workmaster's hearts laundry, cleaning who he can reach in mysterious ways, like a single Bud, making softies as he goes along without knowing.

Uncle Raphael gave a side glance and a wink at Asha, enjoined his niece to a lovely carefully laid table in the middle of the room, and replied to his henchman,

-Well, something is sprouting in your chest, most definitely, Azryel. I did not order. I proposed to your own will. And from seeing Walter's dog, you, as well, are ready to raise eight guard dogs out of a possible minimum of five...your own choice went for the highest number of puppies...mmm...As long as I do not end up with hell dogs at the end of your training, I would love to see this. Dinner is there. Let's eat.'

(verse 22: Eat It All.)

'Raphael smiled and advised,

-Interesting point. I can see that Azryel managed to get under your tits, Babe. He has that effect somehow with everyone. But I'd rather you made sure that your words are good enough and useful to us. As unfortunately, my henchman can show you how a rat can fall further down, by removing any rags it holds onto. He can show any rats a bad time with great pleasure, from a gutter trip to a river drowning trip, to a stripping rags, flesh and muscles strip. Palatable to none but his taste! Do you really want to cater for his taste-buds tonight?

Caroline looked with dismay at her uncle, struck by his clear warning. If she was not so starving, and not shitting herself with fear, she would have stood up and thrown the massive soup container upon Azryel's laps or face, whichever would hurt more. But she tried to remain as impassive as she could and dipped the bread into her soup with shaky fingers, as she finally answered,

-I intend to remain in one piece for my son and Walt, thank you very much, uncle. I will talk. Do not worry about that, without any pin cushion torture or drowning one, for that matter. I just wonder how both of you can sleep at night?

Raphael grinned wickedly and replied amused,

-I don't. I sleep during the day.

Caroline gave him her most irresistible yet unwilling smile and shook her head in disapproval. Her querying eyes remained transfixed by the deep seriousness of the henchman's dark gaze, as he broke a crab claw within one of his hand, making a chilling noise doing so, as he dared to smile back to her with his answer,

-I can never sleep. Done far too much to ever be allowed to do so.

An unnerved Caroline ate a chunk out of her dipped bread, then with her mouth full in a very impolite manner, commented,

-That's very disturbing. You do realise that do you, Mortimer? No human can survive without sleep, for very long without going insane. That would explain a lot.

Azryel ate the crab meat straight from the claw, with his hands, licking his long fingers regularly, in an unconcerned and annoying fashion, his intense gaze maintaining the one of Caroline,

-That I am inhuman and insane. Those are facts, and not to dwell on. Friendly warning, number two.

Caroline pestered across the table, and handed her crab claw to him,

-Blast! Stop licking your fucking fingers! Get some meat out of my food, so I can stop looking at you with ravenous eyes, mad henchman. I beg you, please. And just for the record, I am well past beyond warnings. I already love a mad man. And I truly hope you lot can help my rat of a husband, my Walt, and my big Bro.

The three men laughed out loud, and Azryel took the claw, broke it in one go within his palm and spread carefully the meat upon a little white plate which he handed back to Caroline. He told in a soft encouraging fashion,

-Well. At least we just had a few truthful words from you, Mademoiselle. Carry on, please, we are most eager to know about It-666.'
(verse 22: Eat It All.)

'She giggled pitifully and tears pricked in her eyes. Azryel stood up, started clearing the table, and told in an appeasing and reassuring fashion,

-I will not touch your body in a torturing way even if ordered to, Mademoiselle Caroline. I can hear Workmaster through you. You made your point and your case, vividly clear and it is a valid one. However, and my only correction, is this, your uncle was right about It-666 affecting you through the dog. You are right and said the truth, and I quote you to show your own limitation, 'As you lived at your door'. I know what he said to be so for having assessing you and the dog. But we also do know the fact is certain for the Beast, herself admitted to it to Gabriel, over the phone, she wanted to give you a nice rest after all your hard

work, with no true harm in mind. If the dog had to be told to wake up, in order to make Gabriel's plan work, for you, it was much gentler, by sun rise tomorrow after a good night sleep, you would have woken up by yourself. It was very safely done, with your welfare in mind.

Caroline looked upon him with slight confusion. Maybe the henchman had kindness after all, she dared to think. His comments were picked up by Raphael, who closed his hand into a fist and hammered the table once and soundly, and demanded,

-Azryel, I order and you obey without discussion. How good would you be otherwise?

The henchman carrying on taking the empty dishes, shrugged his shoulders and replied with a huge grin upon his face,

-I think it would make me very good, very good indeed, to all, but probably not to you.

Asha couldn't help smiling back and told with utter disbelief,

-What did got into you, Az? You are a born torturer.

Azryel filled the glass of all with more red wine before confessing,

-All I know is someone was born to kill and doesn't. All I know is that Gabriel has a civilised Beast under his roof, who has gently put someone to sleep soundly just to ask us to kill her. All I know is that I will be asked to do the task if it has to be, like any torturing around this house, or any punitive killing. And all I want to do is if I am a born torturer, is to try the ways of the Beast, and see if they truly work, to experiment them upon me the harshest one there is around, if I can be...

Raphael sighed deeply, and finished his sentence,

-With a heart. You will end up with the same conscious turmoil, begging for your own death.

Asha stood up all of a sudden, stating, while dishing out the dessert to everyone,

-There is the order. And Death has to be. Azryel, willing or not you have to cut it, otherwise we as a whole, will have to do it.'
(verse 22: Eat It All.)

'-I feared you, all, from almost the start. Are angels to be feared? As for you, Asha, strong and peaceful Asha, your own kind, fears you. I gathered you were a killer and a torturer, so how can you be an angel?

Azryel turned back to face her and considered her as she fidgeted, fright growing irresistibly within her, as she was concerned to have dared a little too much by her questions. He remained impassive, took a silver box from the pocket of his jacket, one embossed with the skull and cross bones, opened it and asked politely,

-Do you mind me smoking, Mademoiselle?

She blinked at him a few times, cradling her folded legs against her and answered, bemused,

-I don't know why do you ask for my permission. I fear deep down that you can crush me at any point in time without my consideration. Am I right or wrong?

Azryel lit up a long and slim Havana cigarillo, gave her his wicked smile and replied coolly as he leaned back against the railing of the balcony, gazing at her with intensity,

-You would be right. However, all come in good time. So am I to take your fear of me as granting me your full permission to be uncaring in your presence human?

Caroline gasped at him, and considered him as he smoked his cigarillo, pursed his lips in a 'O' and blew out a perfect 'O' of smoke towards her, in a mocking fashion. She couldn't help smiling and coughing in the same time, offended,

-Bloody hell! You are enjoying scaring the living shit out of people do you? This

should not be allowed!

Azryel came to her, tapped gently upon her back and told,

-Calm down and breathe, little woman. I am sorry. Freaking humans a tad is one of my rare pleasures.

Caroline starred at him as he left her sides to lean against the railing and smoked away from her, most peacefully. With his help, she had managed to catch her breath again. Frustratingly he knew exactly how to make someone feel bad and how to make them feel well, and it was frightening. She commented with no hidden irony,

-A tad, is an understatement. You didn't answer my questions. Am I allowed to ask them? Surely, being the niece of Raphael should make me off limit to you?

Taking the cigarillo of his lips, shaking the ashes from it, and extinguishing the incandescent ones fallen upon the ground with his brown leather Richelieu shoe, Azryel stated as an answer,

-No one is off limit from me, Caroline. I am the Death Angel. I bring all lives to an end at their requested times. And you should relax with me a little, because you are not due yet to be picked up. I deal with my own kind just as well and this is why Asha and all the others, even your own uncle, fear me. However among angels, we form strong allegiance, bonds, and partnerships. I bowed to Raphael, submitted to him my powers, and only accept his orders and advice.'
(verse 23: The Angelic Anonymous Apostasy.)

'Raphael cocking his brows with deep interest, demanded,

-Explanations are in order, Death. Did you gather more information?

Azryel went by him and knelt, bowing his head down, folding his black wings neatly upon his back, he smiled while tentatively looking up to the Archangel,

-The little bird has been very forthcoming.

Raphael shifted uncomfortably and quizzed most worried about the happy smile upon his Death Angel,

-And no torture was involved, wasn't it? Your smile always worries me about the humans you have dealt with, and we are talking about my niece...

Azryel blinked innocently his eyes to him, and answered sardonically,

-The very one, you have frightened all night long about me doing just that. Concerned, now, are you? In fact for all I did, for the first time in my eternal life, I have been offered terms of friendship by a human. If that is worth anything, it nonetheless touched me a tad.

All the angels stared upon him as one, some daring to have the ghost of a smile upon their lips. They looked upon each others as if something incredible had just been said or happened. Raphael laid his hand upon the forehead of Death and asked further smiling blissfully,

-Oh, a miracle, indeed, at your doorsteps! Did you accept the human offer of friendship?

The angels looked up upon the Death Angel with their expectations and heart rising sky high, thinking at once that there was hope for everyone. However, Azryel shook his head negatively very slowly, making eye contact with the twelve of them in turn, and watched the hopes written upon their faces sinking gradually into despair. His voice lowered and took a bitter purposeful tone,

-I declined. But I realised I had no offer of friendships during my eternal life, not even from my own kind, the one I fight by. It makes you humble, and the human proposal was said to remain open for a couple of days, for my consideration. So I will consider the human proposal, as no other kindness has ever been made to me, apart the one taking me into servitude.'
(verse 23: The Angelic Anonymous Apostasy.)

'No one checked this room up and I have been wearing gloves in here and staid in the wardrobe most of the time, following Gab's order almost to the letter.

Azryel looked damn serious, nodding his head in slight disapproval, making a series of signs with his hands, he ordered Asha to sweep the room clean from any tell-tale traces of the presence of the human. Then he asked the human in a silently scolding telepathic query,

-Almost? You do know Walter, that I do not like the sound of that. Either you follow orders, either you don't. What did you do, in there which we need to clear-up?

Workmaster gave him an hilarious grin, batting his eyelashes to him, and answered within his mind,

-Nothing that the toilet flush couldn't clear for you. Come, I am only human. I can follow orders up to a certain point. Basic needs, my dear Angel, basic needs.

Azryel hissed between his teeth in a low voice, looking at his silver Rolex *and showing it to the man,*

-What are you, a bloody toddler? Nine till twelve thirty. When we say, you don't move from one spot that is what you will do, and you will wait until the relief come.

Walter shrugged his shoulders and teased in a whispering pestering tone,

-Right, if that please you better, next time I will let you find me with my arse dipped into its own shit.

The Angel smiled wryly, replying by telepathy,

-That would not be the first time, Workmaster. You have quite a reputation among Us as a shit maker and stirrer, the ace of it. But with me stepping in, my dear human, the order of the day is going to have no laxity whatsoever. Whatever you want to do, you will have to hold it until it is right by me.' (verse 25: COMA, just a stroke not a Final Point.)

Asha.

From all of Raphael's Angels, Asha is one with a very kind heart and the patience of a true Angel. He will take the time to explain things to the lay human without being ordered to do so. He will offer his shoulders without being asked. Known as the 'Philosopher', he has a calm, poised and understanding attitude about him.

That extremely well educated bouncer of an Angel, with affable polite manners, takes his seat at Wrath's table along with Azryel. Which is all the better, for between the hot headed Archangel and the cold blooded Death Angel, his warm heart brings the temperature of the room or conversation down or up to the right level.

Seasoned warrior, reliable soldier, intelligent mind and a kind heart are the stamps on his Angelic passport which made him reach the honour to eat and serve at the table of Raphael, like Azryel does. There is a little more than that, he makes it into the big league fighting wise. He bestows the recognition of Wrath and Az.

We do not know how long it took him to achieve that status, yet what we do know is that Asha is a character full of wisdom acquired along his eternal angelic path. He is well regarded and appreciated by his peers.

Not only that his general, Azryel, himself would mourn him endlessly if that particular Angel lost his life. Death is fond of that invaluable soldier and most descent Angel. The way, that proves he does so, is by his severity and extreme scrutiny towards Asha. This is one Angel, Az would protect the soul of, from any silly mistakes that could cost him his wings.

The best sign of the high esteem the Death Angel regards Asha, is that when Ash proposed to him his friendship at the same time of Raphael, Az accepts Asha's one straight away while putting the other one's request under consideration. Although in that scene,

Azryel plays a bit like a neglected diva on the mind of Archangel Raphael with the definite intention to make Wrath feels bad, he honestly and earnestly welcome the friendship offer of Asha readily, not to prove a point to Raphael and square any petty feud the two constantly have, but because Az is much honoured that such a good soul and descent Angel such as Ash would appreciate his own partly damned and fearsome soul's friendship.

The fact that Asha knows deep down why Azryel behaves like he does and understands the strong life saving principles behind him shows his up-most comprehension of the Death Angel. Asha also words his understanding out loud, which makes a hell of an Angel, like Death, feels that his tough devotion to his Army is definitely not lost on that soldier. It's just reassuringly comforting to know that someone understands you fully. To bestow that person as a friend is a treasure.

The character of Asha is the one of the best friend which will forgive you, stand by you, know where you came from in every aspect all along. You just want to hug Asha, pat his back, or just sit by him and listen to what he has to say. He is one which can teach any about life in a simple manner without arrogant Angelic ways.

We meet this Character many times throughout the saga as he is a main Angel and Soldier of the Angelic Army. I like Asha for his ability to convey to every reader the nitty gritty part of what it feels like to be part of Wrath's Army.

His first name was chosen for two reasons: 'Asha is a Zoroastrian concept of "truth and order"'. I am not a Zoroastrian or belonging to any faith for that matter apart for the one of the human heart, one that dares to be a human above all, which means to simply love, love all.

'Ash', as in his nickname, is also a real person, someone who would not let a stone unturned when a friend of his was victim of racism. Asking for my help and words, he got them, if a letter can make things right, I am mouthy enough to spell out when someone has been wronged. The outcome was happy tidings. Nastiness came to a stop.

Ash is that righteous person which is the true friend that will stand for his friends's sake.
Asha will also spells the right blunt truth and tells you, how bleak or good it is at that moment in time. Like if you went dipping your human toe in the ocean, that Angel will warn you of how rough or cold it is, before you go in there.

Let's meet Asha in quotes:

'She saw the man walking faster, depriving her of a chance to apologise. She mumbled for herself, half pestering,

-I am no racist, for Christ's sake, I am black like you, man.

One bouncer behind her, replied to her in a philosophical manner while carrying his load of the wrapped Bud with others,

-Racism is as widely spread as the colour of the rainbow, unfortunately, it reaches any skin tones you can imagine. It is actually a prejudice to believe that a white would be more racist than you on account to his skin colour. Like the rest of us, the poor bugger didn't get to choose his/her parents and his/her receiving culture at birth. Now righteousness, love, fraternity and open mind is a culture of the heart available to all to transcend and go beyond their disparities and differences. The question anyone should ask themselves is if they did create boundaries in the landscape of their hearts, like humans created boundaries all over Earth, making it a dis-figuration, a war-zone doing so. For in reality there are no boundaries. You can cross a river, a sea, an ocean, a mountain range, a desert, and find your perfect home beyond them. For all you know Mademoiselle Caroline, the ancestral genes of his grand mother might be linked to yours, with all your due respect. Have you ever read Cavalli-Sforza? I highly recommend it. It is a sword through the dragon of racism.'
(Verse 20: Uncle Raphael: Who's the Daddy?)

'He presented her his arm again, and invited her to follow him,

-I have been told to show you to your room. You will be able to retrieve yourself

a little in there. The dinner will be ready in an hour and a half. You can have a good shower in the meantime, but Azryel recommended me to run the Jacuzzi instead for you, on sea mode, with Dead sea salt, lavender and rosemary essence to restore your tired muscles. Forty-five minute to one hour minimum in it, will manage to relax your strained mind from all the events of today and yesterday, he said. He has no doubt that with a good hearty meal, you will manage to sleep like a baby tonight, especially if you tell all to your uncle without reservation, as it will bring you peace of mind too.

Caroline got up and taking the arm most willingly confided,

-I must admit that what he says sounds good and that for once I might just do as I am told. That was kind of him now, wasn't it? I am sure he cannot be that unforgiving.

Asha gave a sad smile, as he confided,

-And you would be wrong, Miss Caroline. Azryel has an acute knowledge of bodies. When he helped you from your fainting spell, he assessed yours. He knows exactly how to make them, and how to restore them, in a very frightening manner. However even if his cold advice is always devoid of kindness and feelings, sound it remains and to do as he says always goes a long way, especially if we don't want to see him across our paths.'
(Verse 21: Tell me all abut It)

'Raphael looked upon him, his face saddened, and confessed,

-They were, Az. Dished out shame by a human at breakfast is rare. After our meeting and your subsequent scolding of Ash, you disappeared all morning, Death, preferring the company of a dog to mine. I would not and can't have you stirred beyond belief by words.

Asha corrected him, putting his breakfast before Raphael,

-Not words, promises, bonds that links one heart to another, a vow of care, friendship is all about caring, and feelings. You care how I feel, and I care how you feel. It is simple and beautiful. Denying it to one of us is atrocious. The

mere fact that Death is a feeling Being should have granted him our consideration of friendship at some point in time, and the human is right about that. I know I wouldn't be corrected so much by Az if he didn't give a fuck about me making it fights after fights. My friendship is granted to him even if he dismisses it. Mademoiselle Caroline, what would you have for breakfast after your uncle Raphael's smile, because I can assure you that it is definitely gone and replaced by serious concern?'

(Verse 24: Helios, Heli-cop-ters, Hell and I)

Liz Arczy.

We meet the character of Liz Arczy briefly in the first book. She then develops slowly but surely throughout the saga to a certain potency and consequence. Receptionist at the clinic of Gabriel, the red head human picked the interest by her quirky personality.

Her first ambiguity lays in the fact that she is a most sociable loner. You can rightly ask me how does that work or what do I mean by that. Liz is a character whose work involves greeting and meeting an array of strangers everyday and her bright smile, conversation bring them the ready comfort that they will be looked after very well in the clinic of Gab. Not only that lively Liz has a very messy after work partying and else, life with again almost strangers. She is there fully surrounded in bars, clubs and wheresoever she enjoys spending her spare time. She mingles and muddles with any, yet her heart will not get involved. If her social going out mates and would be friends loves her to bits, if Liz would give carelessly inches of her body to almost anyone she would not remember in the morning, her heart remains un-given. She protects it fiercely from being hurt, hence she stays well away from love. Liz never did let someone close to her heart since her very unhappy childhood, when her mother gave her up for adoption aged four...

This character lives a singleton life in the fear of what others can do to her if she starts loving them. Some foster parents she liked so much, gave her away just like her mother did, despite her trying her best to please them. The abandon, the hurting rejection, taught Liz the tough lesson to never trust anyone but her own self. The only one who could truly care about herself was just her and no one else.

She became a self reliant woman, who looks very strong and happy on the outside yet who walks upon her achilles's heels ready to tumble to her doom at any point. Worst, the rejection of others, she mirrored it on how she looked after her own self. Devoid of loving care since ages, the character does not know how to look after herself properly. For example, she does not know what a full fridge looks like, nor what a proper meal consists of. She perpetrates on herself how she was always treated. A single glass of fruit juice is the perfect breakfast for her, a packet of crisps the perfect lunch, and if she has dinner it would be a takeaway pizza, just a slice of it and she will give the rest to the homeless guy living in her street.

There is a bit of 'Holly Golightly' in Liz, yet far less glamorous. For a start the character doesn't care that much about her appearance. She lost the care about pleasing others: making efforts results in being abandoned anyway like it did with her many parents, real or foster. She looks like a 'Boho chic' chick, with red messy hair and the attire to fit the bill. However that woman has nothing to do, apart being herself to be just loved by others, especially male counterparts. There is something about Liz that attracts them like night butterflies which she will burn away from her sight and life as soon as she awakes to daylight.

Strong and fragile at the same time, her character has to account for her second ambiguity. I would say myself that she is falsely strong and strongly fragile. She went through much in her childhood and it determined her as an adult, with bases which are far from being universal. If Liz Arczy fiercely looks after herself to keep her very independent lifestyle, she undermined herself with her unhealthy ways. Her feeding habits are anorexicaly appalling. So much so that Liz almost constantly looks like a starved kid that desperately need to be fed. Combined to that her binge drinking, her chain smoking, and wild sex life and you have a recipe for disaster in a woman no taller than 5 foot 1 past her thirties.

She seems to have a fully enjoyable social life but Miss Arczy has been a sad kid, deep down, since a long time. It takes only Angels to know the right truth of the matter. Appearances can't full them long, especially when they are expert mind readers like some of them.

Let me reveal nuggets of news which are happening further down the line in the saga.

First we get to know little titbit's of angelic info. Like any human, Liz was supposed to have a Guardian Angel, yet her unlucky self possessed one who walked away from his duty to devote himself to a demon, far back down her life line. To Angels' eyes, this explains to them the messy life of that unguarded human. She had no protection or advice to prevent her from falling from one bad adventures to another. However this does not excuse the frail woman for humans are granted free will for Angels can only influence them subtly.

Second, the rather celibate Doctor Purallee likes the blunt honesty of Liz Arczy and her person very much. Working with her for years, six to be exact, for she was the replacement of Wendy Workmaster at the reception of the clinic, the Archangel comes to realise that that particular human for some reason is devoid of a Guardian Angel. Already looking after Walter, Caroline and his nephew Micky, what he calls his humans, or his human family, therefore having his hands rather full, Walter Workmaster is a heavy weight of a human to look after, the generous Gabriel nonetheless decides to loosely keep an eye on Liz. As her boss, he checks upon her. Any of her absences and sicknesses, will have him investigating and make sure that she is alright. Him and Caroline will go to Liz's flat offering either their medical help, or their moral support. Gabriel feels he is the personal Doctor of all his employees, but more than that for Liz, there is a latent impression that he could contemplate the human as a potential partner. That secret care of Liz Arczy, if very reserved, almost silently done, with that slight tint that possible love could develop between them one day, is shown touchingly in one gesture that Gabriel only reveals to his Uncle Raphael and Azryel. Knowing how the human lacked vision for her own future, with the same applying to Walter, knowing that both are neither the insurance policy types, nor thinking of provisioning for their older days, the Archangel monthly and secretly puts aside money for this two humans to cover any eventuality that could affect them. He did so for years. He does make sense that he does it for Walter, his family, but for Liz, it tells of a generous somewhat affection for the woman.

Third, for the juicy revelation, Liz simply and literally falls for Azryel Mortimer, the Death Angel. Her brash ways of being did pick the interest of Death. All at once, he is rather amused and saddened by her. He knows her fate, and it is not a rosy one at all, the human has done so much to herself that the curtain of death will draw upon her in give or take six months time from their second meeting. For him, she is the walking pity of a human yet he is touched by her simply faulty humanity. If he is rightly pissed off by a human that is wasting herself away, by sheer indulgence, negligence, and total lack of love, he can not help being taken by her human plight somehow. When he offers her his help and friendship, he receives a bombshell back, a burning one, the gift of Liz's love... To know how this will end you just have to turn the pages of the books of the saga.

Writing the love story between Az and Liz has been a very emotional enjoyment and pure pleasure. From their first look to the build up to the end, their love touches me by its playful yet serious intensity. I will mourn the character of the very mortal Liz, just like her Death Angel when I will write her last lines.

For the trivia, Arczy, her surname was created by rearranging the letters of the word 'Crazy' Her first name had to finish with a Z while her surname had to start with a A for the character represents the A to Z guide of how to mess up your life as a human, the ultimate road map for anybody to go downhill with all the clever shortcuts that reduce years to arrive at your ultimate destination. It is definitely a crazy thing to do to oneself to not care for your own life. And yes for the imagery that would make you a very strong contender to only belong to death. Liz embracing the Death Angel without question is an allegory as much as a love story within the entire saga.

I sometimes inspire myself from real people to build my characters, I dived into my own dirt to write about Liz Arczy. That character bestows a lot of my idiosyncrasies. If I do not indulge in the big craze for selfies, writing Liz was a bit of a self portrait. However I can reassure you that I had a decently happy childhood rather than a sad one. That part of the character's life is just pure creative imagination. Her tendency to swear a hell of a lot is however one of my own bad habits for example. If you would pinpoint me upon it, I would only apologise with a 'scuse my French'. I would feel I would not be able to be myself if I could not do so.

I will not tell you in detail what are the bits describing me from which are not, for writing that character was exposure enough for me. The people that knows me best will recognise them and that is enough of an incentive to deal with.

For the very same reason I will leave Liz Arczy totally unquoted in the Compendiums. If you want to meet her and part of me read the It-666's saga.

The Tutor.

What can I say about that character?

That you will never be able to quite grasp The Tutor even with your best intentions and most clever brain cells fully switched on. Elusive yet fully on, it is a whimsical idea of God, a pure allegory.

I must confess that it is one of my hardest characters to write about. He is the Sum of all Souls. You may find him beguiling. You may find him intimidating for he is. However whenever he steps in, he brings immediate relief with his presence. However he is the one the Angels will seek out to resolve their issues and dilemmas. Daunting, mysterious, knowing more than he will reveal at any one time, talking almost with riddles and puzzles to work out, he is the hard core of entities.

Our young Beast ran into him age five, straight after she killed her first humans, the murderers of the nun Tess who was looking after her. He calmed her little Being right down, soothed her distraught soul until she slept at his feet. He is the one, the Being, that kept her in the Black Forest after the two humans who hid the Beast there to protect humanity, passed away. He preserved their good work alive and well with his instructions. She was free to run wild as long as she remained in the forest.

The three years the Beast lived feral in that forest remains an entire mystery, however we know that she calls the Sum of all Souls, her Tutor, that she has great respect for him, that she will kneel by him without being forced to or asked, it is almost an impulse to do so for her. We also know that he appeared to her feral self regularly, kept an eye upon her, but more importantly educated her in a Being sort of way.

Between five and eight, the Beast was not solely a lone soul in the depth of the Black Forest. She had that important visitor meeting her footsteps teaching her as if she was a young Angel. He impressed upon her mind greatly. Despite not knowing about his tuition, we are aware that it was special enough for It-666 to never kill any human even when she was put under tremendous torture between age 8 and 16. The Beast was steadfastly strong and good, unwilling to use her lethal powers and hiding them from human eyes despite being hurt physically to make her show them. She rather prefers her own death. Age 16, we find her, like Walter in that appalling state, having braved all kind of tortures, with for only hope in her mind to be dead and buried to present no threat to humanity.

What can I say about the Tutor? He was an important part of the childhood of It-666. He was the first Being, she ever met, one who taught her how to control herself and her powers. Not totally for the little Beast failed to complete her instruction... Despite being told by him to stay away from humans and to stay safely in the forest like all beasts should, her lonely eight year old self ran to meet school children to befriend them on their school trip in her forest. Herald as a feral child by their teacher, mocked for her strange voice by the children, It-666 was taken out of her cherished Black Forest, her home of eight years to be put in a psychiatric hospital under observation. Abducted from there, flown to the US, she ended in a cage for a bedroom under a pentagram made of human blood in Paul Peterson's Bunker for eight long years of endless torture.

When the Angels discover It-666 at the start of the saga, the Tutor is already aware of her existence, not only that far from destroying her, he educated the youngster. Food for thought for all Angels, especially for Wrath for the Tutor is his 'Master', the one he answers to. However he was not made aware by him about the existence of the Beast whatsoever nor was he told about her loss from the Black Forest. He was not asked to recover her at all cost. He did not know that the daughter of Eremiel even walked upon earth at that time. The discovery of her Being comes into the light when she is sweet sixteen when Walter Workmaster pulls her out of her cage.

This begs the question what did the Tutor achieve by keeping It totally secret even from his Angels? Was it a 'watching how the little Beast would react' scheme to know if she could be trusted? We will never know. However what we are aware of is his interest about her. He is a character with an agenda of his own, which he will never disclose to others. His orders are transmitted to Wrath, who spreads them to all Angels, but also to something called 'the Powers'. The Tutor deals with a lot but the way he does it, remains unseen. However, the way Wrath intervenes for him, has such impact that all feel his force in the background.

We meet the character throughout the saga many times, mainly in times of needs for all other characters, emphasising his parallel to a god like figure. They seek his help at the last resort. It is always not a given, it is always hard to get. They really have to plead the creed of their own paths to him.

Let's meet him in quotes and passages:

'Before the Death Angel could say a word in reply, a voice sang a very sad, powerful and peaceful lullaby. Azryel scrutinised his surrounding, yet could see nothing. It-666 was up on her feet at once, joy passing through her green eyes, where resignation reigned before. She took the hand of Death, inviting him to follow her,

-He is here! Come, meet my Tutor. Come, I know where he is, very close by, where he taught me many things...

Azryel ran with her intrigued to finally be able to discover the face of the Angel who took on the young Beast. They reached a small clearing with a great oak tree almost in its centre, and below it stood a Being glowing powerfully. The young It left his hand to run towards him. The Death Angel considered the whole scene. When the teenager reached the Angel, she knelt by him, putting even her head upon the floor, she obviously had a relationship with him that could not be described by simple words. He truly believed at that moment, that It-666, the Beast, the due Antichrist was worshipping her 'former' Tutor. But who was he? The question was crucial as if he was worshipped by It, it also meant his influence upon her could be great. This could pose problems to Raphael, Gabriel and him in the guardianship of the young Antichrist.

The first words of the Being teased gently It-666, as he stroked her cheeks in the most gentle and kind manner,

-Here, here, brave girl, you are doing well. I never thought my instructions would impress you so much, my little Beast in the woods.

Az could not help but be impressed by the awe which clinched him deep down by the sides of that Being. He was no Angel, for that he was sure of, he was something else, something else but what? Who? Death stood full of suspicion and asked It,

-Bambi, too much effusion. Stand up, by me and do the presentation.

She smiled at him in a childlike manner,

-Azryel Mortimer, Angel of Death, meet my Tutor.

He grinned a little annoyed replying with slight impatience,

-And your tutor has a name, I suppose?

The Being gazed upon Azryel attentively as he replied instead of It calmly and firmly,

-It, chose 'It' to be her name for the time being, until she finds her own one, not a satirical one given by others. As for Ours We have many.'
(verse 31: The Tutor)

'The Tutor put his hand upon Death's arm recalling him,

-Lets move on to another chapter of It's childhood. The child saw you somehow. You don't want to be exorcised, do you bad spirit?

Azryel smiled sarcastically, as he answered,

-How would you know if I was a bad spirit? Anyhow I can not be erased for I do the erasing in every Worlds.

The Being smacked his hands together bringing the three of them to a new scenery after mentioning,

-A self satisfied spirit can be a plague and also a plague to deal with. Ask Raphael, he will tell you the same for he knows.'
(verse 31: The Tutor)

'Azryel, the Death Angel was by now annoyed with the Tutor for he seemed to know far more than him. Transported to another moment in time in the childhood of It-666, three years forward, he wondered if he would be able to gather the identity of their guide. Death enquired,

-You seemed to know me very well yet I did not have the privilege of your acquaintance. Do you personally know Archangel Raphael?

The Tutor beaming blinding light throughout his entire entity replied nonchalantly, ignoring the fact of how disturbing he was at that moment,

-We made a point to know all. There is no bright sides nor dark ones that are escaping Us. We know you Azryel Mortimer very intimately and so do We know General Raphael.

The Angel shook his head in an helpless fashion before raising it with a sarcastic smile,

-Many Names, either you are the most pedantic Being in the whole World, either you are the sum of all spirits to adopt the universal we speaking of yourself. Which is it?

Winking at the Death Angel, the Tutor replied pointing at the three year old It-666 running happily in the forest,

-Take a wild guess. You are getting closer.'
(verse 32: Soulful Singing lark.)

'Death felt the teenage It-666 holding his hand as the infamous scene of her past appeared. He could feel her hand trembling within his. She confided to him,

-Azryel, I don't know if I am ready to see this part. I might get upset all over again and react. I may need to be contained.

The Tutor turned to her, his voice soothing and strong reassuring her at once,

-My little lost beast We taught you how to contain your own self, your wrath and desire of retaliation. We know you can do it for you are Our brave one. Be confident as you have shown great restraint which honours your every action ever since that event. You can rely upon your own self forever, remember that as a fact. You can win your own inner battle yourself. Never forget that. Never. You are stronger that the rest of Us. You cannot give your own responsibilities to anyone great or small for it will wreck them all. Remember your own internal turmoil, its your own to deal with, it has been given to the most powerful Being ever for good reasons. It cannot be shared. It can be dealt with, by you and you only. We are counting on you to do so. We will walk by you all the way to help you support your ordeal. You can count on Us to not let you fail. What you are about to see, you have grown out of it. You have become the courageous individual We always knew you would be. Against all odds, you made it to the AA Army as their newest recruit. And for all you are, It, they need you more than you will ever know in the future that is unfolding as We speak.

The Death Angel felt the hand of It-666 becoming strong and firm. Her trembling disappeared during the arousing speech, he had noticed. Somehow he wished he had told her all those exact words at that moment in time. Somehow he wished that someone could care enough of his own self to come up with spurring words like those to carry on his own eternal task or the courage to give it up. He looked bereft upon the Tutor who was beaming bright like a beacon within the Black Forest. By now Azryel knew who was 'Many Names', the Tutor of the Beast and he could hardly believe it. Was The Most Superior Being of All truly there for all creatures?'
(verse 33: Tess's Death.)

Theresa Da Priera, aka Nun Tess.

Nun Tess was the tough catholic sister who abducted the Beast at her birth on the 6th of June 1996 with Father Williamson. She is the one that took charge of her care up until It-666 was five years old. On the fifth birthday of the Beast, she was killed ruthlessly before her by men paid to abduct the child.

We do not know much about Nun Tess apart that the Portuguese was some sort of surrogate mum to It-666, one that would exorcise 'the child' every night. Tess was almost the first contact of the Beast with a human if we remove the hands of father Arthur Williamson who assisted at her birth and put her in the Nun's arms, still with an umbilical cord attached to her demonic goddess of a mother to be cut.

Tess is a nun on a mission to save humanity like Father Williamson whom she takes orders from. Like him she is a fervent Christian. Like him and other catholics, she participated in cursing the Beast whilst still in the belly of Lilith. They cursed the Beast to have a heart, not in the physical organ aspect but in the moral sentiments one. They succeeded as It-666, 'The child' as Tess calls her, shows signs of having a good sensitive heart.

The nun educate It-666, teaching her how to read and write. The Beast's school books have the delicious irony of being the bible and the lives of Saints. Bright, she learns abnormally fast. The Child also possess a characteristic which unsettles the nun slightly, she has the capacity to express herself in any language. She seems to know all of them without having to study them.

Tess is a strong character who did influence It-666 from an early age. Despite the demonic capacities of the child, she impressed on her enough to be good and to fight her demons.

The Tutor, when he first learnt of the existence of the Beast, and where It was hidden, went with the firm intention of killing Eremiel's child. However as he observed Tess and her interactions with the Beast, he realised the good work the humans had done in cursing her and raising her up. It was not necessary to erase the Beast from the surface of the Earth. His intentions then changed to strengthen the work of the nun and secure the Being of It-666 on her path of remaining good.

Tess had achieved something important by her looking after of the Beast. She helped determine her sweetly strong character that aimed to stay good. If the curse sowed the seeds by giving a heart to the child of evil. The nun cultivated that heart to make it go in the right direction. All the Tutor had to do, was adding his support to the young tender Being.

The name of the character was created in reference to my own ancestors and family. However it is a blend of a few individuals within it. Therese is the first name of one of my aunts, widow with five children, she had an endless energy to bring up her children. She was a tower of strength for them, like Theresa is taking on the responsibility of raising up the little Beast. For Da Priera, my grandfather was Portuguese, and I used part of the surname of his mother which was Jesus Da Priera. The fact that Tess is from Portugal is not a mystery. It is a wink to some of my roots. As for the fact that she is regarded as a Saint by the Angels, that she has that strong religiously soldiering persona about her, was inspired by Ste Marie Madeleine Postel who is one of my ancestors. I would say that Nun Tess character has been composed to show a strong woman, with deeply rooted religious beliefs. Nothing scares her, she will attempt to thwart the evil plan of Eremiel with his conception of the Beast, by insuring with others that she is born with a heart. Then she will cultivate that heart, by raising 'It'. The simple human answer to 'It' is just 'Love'. With love, you resolve everything, with hate you destroy all that lives. The entire saga contains that message and statement.

Now what happens in the early years of the Beast, from her conception to when we meet her in book one of our Saga, 'Finding It-666', age sweet sixteen, in her cage under a pentagram, will be released in a prequel trilogy. So Nun Tess will be seen again big time, as one of the main characters of the prequel.

Until we meet her again, let's travel back in time and get a good glimpse of her,

'Death followed the gliding Tutor across the clearing where he pointed to him the path of the great deer. An untouched snow was glistening under the last rays of the cold afternoon sun for him to acknowledge. Walking behind the fast moving Being Azryel was eager to discover more. Soon they reached a little log cabin in the midst of the wood, the Being pointed to a nun and a priest carrying an infant in his arms, walking silently in the snow towards the cabin.

The Tutor announced to It and Azryel,

-This is the arrival of It-666. She is just six month old. The priest holding her tight is Father Arthur Williamson, and the nun is Sister Theresa Da Priera. Both were there at the birth of the child. Take a closer look at It. Remember, none can see you.

Death approached to be at arm distance only from the priest and watched in wonder. The baby was extremely beautiful with a head covered by lovely blond curls, like a cherub, yet as she opened her eyes staring right at him the picture perfect was immediately destroyed. She had deeply black and braising demonic eyes. She blinked a few times, smiled at him then waved, blabbering,

-Az, Azry, Az.

The priest thrust her back more closely into his chest, telling to the Sister,

-She is seeing things again. Let me warn you Tess that you will never be completely alone with her. Spirits, demons and ghosts will be surrounding you at all times.

To which the nun replied shrugging her shoulders,

-Well any entities better be warned I will not suffer their presences around the little one. I will exorcise them all.

The Tutor put his hand upon Death's arm recalling him,

-Lets move on to another chapter of It's childhood. The child saw you somehow. You don't want to be exorcised, do you bad spirit?

Azryel smiled sarcastically, as he answered,

-How would you know if I was a bad spirit? Anyhow I can not be erased for I do the erasing in every World.'
(verse 31: The Tutor)

'They witnessed the special toddler as she found a lark lying lifeless on a layer of leaves. Carefully picking the little song bird up within her baby hands, she considered it attentively. A few pokes from the child had no effects. She kissed tenderly the feathers and ran back towards the cabin with her new found feathery treasure. She showed her find to the Sister who was cutting wood into logs with a large axe. The nun Theresa rose her eyebrows and scolded her,

-No, child, you can not bring every dead thing in the house. We have a garden now filled of those dead animals. If you ever bring me a live creature I may let you keep it as a pet, but that would imply you looking after it and caring for all its lifetime and at three, I doubt you are up to it right now. Did you kill that one or found it like that?

The toddler blabbered away,

-Like that. I heard it sing. In the morning. Every morning singing song. Nice. I want the little bird back.

Theresa dropped her axe by her side and held the child's hands together, enclosing the lark within. She stated,

-The little bird flew away into the spirit world. Maybe it was its time, maybe it had an accident. The wind was powerful last night. Who knows. Feel its cold breast, its little heart has stopped. It means is life is totally over and will not sing anymore, despite us wanting it to do so. It passed away to our great sadness but maybe it made babies this year, who will sing next year.

The little It-666 started crying gently her baby blood tears, and mumbled,

-I wanna hear his babies but I wanna hear him too. I wanna hear his little heart again. I wanna have him all back and alive.

The Sister took back her axe, lifted it and told,

-Cry all you want, child. It is life. With life comes an inevitable death. And all your wants and 'wanna' can do nothing about it.

The young curly blond girl pouted. She shook her head, spoke in tongues for a minute then reverted back to the human language for the benefit of the nun, in her strangely odd voice,

-I can do something. For all I want I can. Heart means life you kinda said. Watch.

Theresa dropped her axe at once and her hands went to join the ones of the toddler upon the bird, giving her most disapproving look. She scolded,

-Think before you do anything, child. A heart can beat with its spirit gone. Without its spirit the lark will be a living shadow. Its songs will ring into our ears every morning soulless.

It-666 smiled brightly at the nun. She stroked the lark upon her own heart and whispered,

-I can feel what you mean. It is not far away. I can catch it back too. I got it. I got it right there with the heartbeats.

She opened her hands to release a living lark. The bird flew to a tree nearby, sang beautifully before flying back to the child landing on her shoulder. The Sister muttered to herself,

-I will be damned, the child Antichrist can make miracles, age three.

Death looked at the Tutor for answer yet he was enjoined to keep his whole attention upon the scene,

-It is far from over.

Azryel saw the toddler running to the garden plot by the cabin. There she dug and unearthed dead animals. One by one she raised them all from their dying state back to the living. When all were running happily around her, she laughed out loud and tried to reassure the deeply worried and baffled Sister,

-They are all good. They are all okay, they all got their souls back too.'
(verse 32: Soulful Singing Lark.)

'Azryel focused back upon the scene as he saw Sister Theresa opening one window of the cabin happily, humming a joyous air. Death recognised the 'Do-Re-Mi' tune of the 'The Sound of Music' film and sadly shook his head when he saw the doomed human putting a strawberry cake to cool upon the window sill.

He whispered to the Tutor,

-The strict nun loved the child. She was celebrating her fifth birthday. I understand they hardly had any food yet she managed to get enough to bake a cake and finishing it off by using strawberries from their small garden.

The Beaming Being replied,

-They looked after each other. The 'child' remained the child for the nun. Sister Theresa did not enforce upon It-666 a monstrous identity. She treated her as a child first and foremost, a special one that needed to be told upon not to make zombies in the garden patch. Yet she tried to educate her too, like any child to write and read. She realised soon enough the 'child' already knew that, and more frighteningly so she knew it in all languages, alive or dead. Tess exorcised the child every evening since she was one. It worked like a favourite bedtime story to the young impressionable Beast. It made her fight her own evil every night before she could rest peacefully exhausted. Fight against Evil was impressed upon the child first and foremost by Tess. In the young It-666's heart, Sister Theresa is her mother, adoptive and all encompassing of her all specialness. Yet Theresa failed to name the child as she dreaded the day, she would be snatched from her. She expected it to happen. She always thought she would never survive the grief of it. She did not. Watch.

Four men ran within the woods towards the small cabin, fast and fully armed.

The young Beast in her river lifted her head up, shivered all over, the fish within her palms was charred to death. She ran as fast as she could towards the cabin.

When she arrived upon the scene, Sister Theresa had a colt pointed to her head, with four men harassing her. She could not stand the rib cage battering inflicted upon her guardian and shouted to the aggressors,

-I am here. Come and get me.

One staid by the nun as three went to grab the child. Although It-666 went straight to the man holding the colt and no one could stop her.

Theresa pleaded,

-Run away, child. Do not fight. Run away from it all.

The man shouted to the nun,

-Shut up, Bitch! No running away on my watch.

He pulled the trigger of his colt.

Tess closed her eyes, blood pouring from her forehead covering them and whispered her last words, before falling lifeless in front of her,

-Run, far and you will see One's way. Run far away.

It was not to be so, as when the child reached her she enclosed the Sister within her small arms and cried out,

-No..............

The man holding the gun met her braising black demonic eyes just once before bursting into a living human flame. As she turned around to ran away, It met the three others, and her straight look within their eyes sent them bursting into flames likewise. She ran past them further and further away from the fire she was leaving behind her. Her eyes were covered by blood tears, she could barely see her way forward. She started shivering all over as she jumped streams and bushes, as an understanding reached her that she had burned those murderous men alive just by looking at them. The more she trembled, the more she felt the ground below her tremor. It was getting worse the further she went. The sky was dark at three. An electrical storm flashed lightnings by her path, splitting trees until she reached a clearing where the sun seemed to be there despite it all. Breathless she ran to a Being sitting peacefully upon a dead log. He opened his arms wide opened and received her. Patting her back, he started singing to her something she had heard before. It soothed her slowly but surely. The quake by her feet ceased altogether as she fell upon her knees by the Being. She asked him breathless,

-Are you the One? I need to run a bit more if not.

The Being stroked her cheek gently, answering,

-You will always be a runaway, child. Tess called me to look after you, to keep an eye on you for a while longer and forever.

She smiled to him and just collapsed at his feet.'
(verse 33: Tess's Death)

Father Arthur Williamson.

Father Williamson is one instrumental character which changed fate by a simple trick up his sleeve: a curse. To be honest I do not let any readers know much about him at any stage in the saga. Although if we meet him again in book 3, he is still a short encounter, yet a vital one. However he is one of the main hero of the prequel trilogy to the Saga of the Beast.

Father Arthur Williamson is an Irish catholic priest. This character is never in the foreground or not for long, however like Raphael he is an enterprising puppet master, but of the human kind rather than Angelic. His aim is similar to the one of the Archangel: Save humanity at all cost.

Williamson devised a great plan to plague the up and coming Beast. Father Arthur's ideas were followed by enough humans in a very specific secret society to make it work: It-666 would be a creature born with a feeling heart and a conscience. This is a terrible troubleshooting and predicament for a created monster. Not only that, to reinforce his deed, the Priest added to the mix: nurture and culture, by giving the Beast to Nun Tess to be looked after, with his special instruction on how to raise Eremiel's daughter.

His beautifully simple human way to fight evil does not lack irony. It's a purely art and craft affair which worked so well that it infuriates evil against Father Williamson, to the extent that when caught the Priest faced a torturing death at the hand of Eremiel, followed by his soul being dragged to Hell. Supposedly prisoner of hellish flames for eternity, until he meets the Beast he cursed, fighting down there, now aged sixteen, a soldier of the Angelic Army...

How to describe that influential character?

Arthur is all about creating Heaven upon Earth and preventing Hell to reign upon it. He is a myth, an idea, an hero. He is king Arthur born into a Priest to save humanity.

Imagine someone with long white hair, a piercing hazelnut gaze, tall and somewhat a little corpulent, and you will get close to the vision of Arthur. He has wizard written all over him: Another 'Merlin'. He is someone that you can not track easily. Yet he will pull a fair few triggers unnoticed, making everything move in the right direction.

Father Williamson has engineered the Beast's curse from scratch, but also her abduction, and how to keep her hidden from all. It almost worked, apart that the Beast was found at some point, when he was horrendously tortured and he revealed her whereabout, five years later. The enormity of his simple human plot was from then on in jeopardy. It precipitated the death of Nun Tess. All their hard work and scheme to prevent the destruction of humanity only relied on one individual only: the Child Beast. Did they do enough to secure her heart and character? They did well enough for an Angelic character, the Tutor, to carry on with their project and further 'It''s formative years in a very Being's way.

Like Tess, this character is a very important one in the prequel of It-666 Saga. Whatever steps Arthur Williamson took to protect humanity are simply rewriting the fate of all, from humans to the Beast passing by the one of Angels.
Watch this space.

For the trivia, Arthur is the middle name of someone special who made me step forward in my own life. The magic he employed were just words. Applying those words into practice brought magic into my life, transforming my future. The kind of magic, I am talking about here, is not about stardust sprinkled over your shoulders anointing you, transforming you from toad to prince, no it is more humble and human than that. The one, I am on about is a good conversation, a one to one, words of wisdom that inspire you beyond belief, enough to make you walk into a certain direction more firmly than ever, the one of your inner dreams. It does transform you into who you aspire to be, to become, to do, by telling you about all the human steps it involves.

It is confidence building: 'Yes, humans did walk on the moon. Why would you not realise your dream?'

What is stopping us on our track? Fear, shyness, money, others... Everything can be worked upon.
One thing you must be clear upon is that it is your life. So do you want to be a cork thrown wherever the waves and tides go or upon the surf board guiding it the way you want, with all the thrill of it. Yes you might get thrown from the surf board, yes popping your head out of the rough water in this instance feels so much better, so much more alive than little 'corky' having none of its ways, doing so.

Ask yourself what would you do if you win the lottery, big time. Sometimes, the answer is your true dream. Two years ago, answering to that one, I replied being a full time writer, published author and having my own publishing company. The question hitting me back was simply: 'How would you feel if you have achieved all this without a lottery win?'.

Many smiles (from ironical to genuine passing by disbelief): 'Very good indeed, proud. How would I go about it?'

The coming response was: 'Let's find out together. It is going to be sheer hard work.'

Two years later, I tick two boxes out of my three dreams. Yes, it was sheer hard work: Like being on a 24/7 non stop. Yet, do I feel proud of the achievement? A thousand times yes, I wish my RIP dad would have seen his 'Pupuce' do so well from scratch.

I will never sit pretty and wait for the lottery to make my dreams come true, I will work upon them and make them more concrete and tangible by sheer hard work, one simple step at a time: hard working, may be, rewarding, definitely. But it brought my dreams fast forward to a certainty within two years. Fight the myth that you have to be rich first to live your dreams. The inverse is the reality of the matter. To be rich is not a money matter either. It is a heart one.

Father Arthur Williamson is very much a combination character.

Like my mum would say about herself that she is a 'Tutti Frutti', a cocktail, I can say the same about Williamson. There is a mix of inspiration that created him to his specific blend: a bit of King Arthur, with a good amount of my very real Arthur, and an added dash of Merlin thrown in for good measure like Tabasco in a good 'Bloody Mary'.

I will not provide quotes for that special character in this Compendium. He will be fully revealed when the Prequel goes to publication.

Paul Peterson. Aka 'P'.

As dreadful as it sounds, it's not only Angels that get incarnated... Demons do so just as well, especially if they are fallen Angels gone bad. 'P' is one of them.

As dreadful as he sounds, 'P' is charismatic, a politician aiming for the USA presidency, followed by many, demons and humans alike, shamelessly leaving bones behind him on his big time crime trail which involves worshipping the devil by regular sacrifices.

Dreaded, he is, by his own followers, for 'P' is a driven character that has only his own promotion in mind and will step on all others to achieve what he wants. He will use and abuse all, below or above him to get what he wants. His only cares in the entire world are himself and his ambitions. He will coax and destroy accordingly.

Whatever 'P' decides to inflict always causes a dreaded pain. From the loss of one soul to human sacrifice for his evil worship to having a Being kept in a cage and tortured for eight long years, passing by the minimal gruesome loss of limbs and organs under his hands, 'P' is definitely one you would not wish to meet in reality. He causes damage wherever he passes.

The character of 'P' is the big Bad in the first and second books of the Saga. He is an angelic-Demon who had the momentum to bewitch Eremiel to do his own bidding with the help of a powerful Cambion witch, Cato, not only that he managed to abduct his daughter, the Beast, and he held her in captivity for years. If he did not get anything by torturing the Beast apart for her will to die, what he got from her father was some sort of partnership which involved regular steady murders on his part to feed evil, in order to have in return the political fame he sought.

It brought him a success that would make you shiver with the particulars from how it was achieved, down to his last bill with Eremiel. At the end of book one, we witness a specific sacrificial ceremony, which shows the relations between the two characters. It is unsettling.

However 'P' is just the tip of the iceberg in the cold blooded mountain of the bad arse characters of It-666's Saga. When you start digging about him, you will discover his backers, associates, brothers, and how he breeds a family like a future monstrous Army.

To start we just hear about 'P' by the other characters who have been affected in one way or another by him and his actions: from Walter Workmaster, who lost his twin sister Wendy who was human sacrificed to evil by the incarnated demon, who broke down as a result, losing his job as a human rights lawyer, losing his wife who feared for their little son; to Gabriel Purallee who lost the human fiancee, he contemplated to spend his incarnated time with, filling him with a tremendous grieving guilt, for surely an Archangel like him should have protected Wendy better from that type of demonic murder happening to her poor human self; passing by It-666, the Beast 'P' kept in a cage under a pentagram and tortured for eight long years, leaving her within an inch of life, and so heartbreakingly suicidal that she is ready to give that inch of life away at every opportunity.

The situation of all the characters as we meet them, in their present, in the Fall of 2012 is very much a condensed result of P's doings and tribulations upon Earth. Because of Paul Peterson's murder of Wendy which had occurred 6 years earlier, we meet Walter Workmaster in the first pages of the Saga, as a Private Investigator working at undoing the politician tirelessly to bring him down to justice one day. He follows the cold trails that P is leaving behind him, and investigating his footsteps. His endeavour has the comprehension of his wife Caroline and the strong backing of Gabriel. Workmaster's will to dig up any trash from P to avenge his dead twin made him stumble upon the teenage Beast kept in her own mess in her cage. The Being, clearly a victim of Paul Peterson in Walter's mind, one of his leftover, 'left but not over yet' upon Workmaster's own words, meet his immediate intervention and compassion.

The rescue of It-666 by Workmaster enrage the demon P when he gets to learn about it. He vows to get back 'his' Beast, but also to kill personally the impudent human who keeps putting an investigating nose in his affairs for the past couple of years. Walter Workmaster makes it on top of the hit list of Paul Peterson. When the Archangel Raphael gets involved in the protection of his human and the Beast Workmaster has decided to adopt, he also becomes a target for P on the equal footing of Walt, the top of P's hit list.

However Wrath went straight there for his heavy interventions against Paul Peterson. What Gab and Walt couldn't achieve together by their humble means, he can with his Angelic Army, and his punitive warning ways. He has the skill to force a demon to hide from the surface of the Earth, to push them back to Hell.
You will learn all the details in the second book of the Saga.

Fighting P together cements the strong relationship between the Angels and the teenage Beast. They have a common enemy. It brings them immediately closer. Their coalition starts powerfully by the retrieval of the abducted little Micky. Wrath, Azryel and It work together for the first time to rescue an important incarnated Archangel, the son of Walter.

To resume, P is a character to be dreaded in many ways, the first 'baddy' of the Saga. His wake is followed by other bad arses that can chill your spine, like Cato the Cambion witch, or crush it like Zeus, his brother...

P has a tad of leftover of his Angelic past, however far back it has been since he was an Angel. But this is just a pinch of salt thrown in the ocean of the demon he became. He may give a chance to his victims, a simple ask, order, or advice that if not followed, will lead to their certain death. He will show to some by that mean their chance to live, if they fail to grasp their opportunities, then they are just fair game to him and just his to 'rightfully' kill. He has little care and no remorse, yet he permits himself to judge others or pass comments, like an Angel would.

Writing 'P' was demanding. I hate this character but less than I do with his brother Zeus. You have a complexity with him, the last

Angelic traces within him that are not to be found in Zeus.

Let's meet that bad arse of a demon in quotes:

'In Boston, within the large mansion of famous politician Paul Peterson, the night was not going according to any plan. For no plans went well for the last few days, and the infamous 'P' was seated in a narrow control room watching over and over again the CCTV footage from his bunker. He asked for the hundredth time to the last man standing, the torturer called '3',

-And the all bunker vanished? Demolished by vegetation, rats and mice... And the Beast was there but disappeared, and so was the 'Real' Santa Morte with a big silver scythe and all, and some large winged creature took the child, Workmaster's son, away with it into the air... In my honest opinion, Mister 3, you just went bonkers.

The man stuttered helplessly, and pleaded,

-Lets watch it all again Sir, it must all be there, it must.

Peterson lifted his hand with impatience, as he ruled it out,

-My bunker is gone and I have a mad man as an only witness who does not make sense at all. I am very upset right now Mister 3. All my plans to regain the Antichrist relied on the exchange between Walter Workmaster's son and her. Now I have nothing left, not even the place to keep my Antichrist. Indeed, Mister 3 I am very, very upset. I shall not watch again that fuzz of a CCTV footage. I shall cut your damn tongue and relieve the headache of the bad news it caused doing so.'
(verse 35: Playing P.)

'Peterson was transfixed upon what he saw and asked for it to be replayed, then asked BigBrother4 to stop at one precise moment,

-There, look at the eyes of that kid when the blade of the knife is slashing his wrists. Pause it. Just there, pause it, I said.

3 and BigBrother4 stated at once, together,

-Fire balls. There's fire burning in his eyes.

Paul Peterson laughed out loud,

-And how many kids do you know with that kind of eyes? None, I am sure, that is because we stumbled upon Workmaster's one, and he happens to be a very special one which got rescued big time by paranormal creatures. 3, you have seen enough, lived enough, your time with me has ended.

Mister 3 looked in disarray, pointed at the CCTV's and begged,

-But you saw what I saw.

P stood up as he answered, pressing a red button upon the panel,

-I know and for that very same reason I do not need you anymore. However I will be magnanimous with you, for you shall live yet unable to communicate.

Two henchmen stepped in the room within seconds, as P ordered,

-3 is to lose his tongue and fingers. Get rid of all his identification papers and release him into the wild, far from here. May God take him into his tender care and grace.'
(verse 35: Playing P.)

'P smiled thoroughly back to his Master and replied,

-By gathering all the human parts needed to perform the feat. I have already a few which I was going to offer you as a feeding gift. Now, the parts will play a much more important role. Communication, all what they were intended for. I am missing some which I expect to come forward within a few minutes. The last piece will feed you well for three days.

The figure laughing loudly asked,

-Have you got something up your sleeve?

The Daemon replied with a knowing smirk,

-Human stupidity and vanity as usual Master.

As he finished his words, a small knock resonated within the room, a weak voice tried her luck,

-It is only me, Dumpling. I heard a bad noise. Are you alright?
The dark shadow corked his eyebrows,

-Dumpling? Interesting. My gift, my feed, I suppose?

P replied quickly in a low voice before answering to the knock loudly,

-Yes, Master. An infatuated little posh goose, beautiful and clever, which believes her belly button can make the whole world turn. You will love her blood, fresh, healthy and young.

-Go back to bed Sweetie. I knocked a mirror moving badly. Nothing sensational. Remember what I said to you. Bed. Now.

Marie replied opening the door straight away,

-Aww, poor thing let me make it all better for you.

P shook his head disapprovingly, stated in a low voice for his Master's benefit,

-Here we go, human sheer stupidity. Is it lack of understanding or insolence? I keep wondering as it never fails.

Marie stood in the bathroom and shouted at the sight of her bleeding politician lover. He moved forward and silenced her swiftly. The young woman fell unconscious upon the bathroom floor tiles.
P turned to his Master, with a wicked self satisfied smirk,

-Feeding time, the meat is fresh. Now, I have all the human parts required, ready for the communication ceremony.'
(verse 36: Of Sucking Parts, Blood, and Lives.)

Wendy Workmaster.

Wendy Workmaster is a character which is only mentioned here and there. Wendy is past, gone and dead yet remembered by many with a sore heart, especially her twin brother Walter and her fiancé Gabriel.

How to describe Wendy?
She was another little Walter, a pure Workmaster through and through. She could finish the sentence of her brother and he could finish hers. They would laugh and cry at the same time, at the very same things. Physically, she is a tomboy blond, the exact copy cat of her brother. Very pretty in understated ways, she grabbed the overwhelming attention of Archangel Gabriel.

Her personality is similar to the one of Walter, again: she is one free spirit. She is not afraid to make tough decisions and hit the road when something is wrong. She has her own mind and you shall not make her bow to settle for a prison, even a loving one, if it kept you away from humanity. She is a human, after all and before all.

She had absolutely no idea that the Big Gab, she said 'yes' to, was a big fat Archangel. She found his possessiveness and jealousy totally out of order and she was right for it was. She flew out of the relationship, asking to rethink about her betrothal.

Quiting the reception desk of Gab's clinic, she found a new job as a PA of politician Paul Peterson. Asked to tour the US for his campaign, Wendy follows, taking the opportunity of the road trip to rethink her relationship. Time and space was all she needed to make up her decision with a cool mind. A last phone call made to her reassured Gabriel upon his betrothal and Walt who was helping him to wow his sister back big time. Yet, this was the last time they ever heard her voice.

Wendy never returned to them. She was killed like so many others. Sacrificed upon a pentagram, Wendy lost her life. Her human blood was only shed to feed the greed of evil. Her soul was dragged to

Hell like a token/trophy, kept there with the many other souls claimed by P.

Wendy went to 'Neverland' for her brother Walter, and he broke down knowing she was no more. He wanted to join her, and was stopped by Gabriel to do so, to kill himself, just in time, in front of his young family. What Big Gab found was a brother completely distraught ready to reunite with his twin in the After-life.

Archangel Gabriel threw himself into the care of Walter and his family, after Wendy, in her memory. He is the providing uncle, the one they all can turn to. He has guilt sown to his grief which makes him devote himself to Workmaster's family.

Wendy is a character whose soul will be rescued from Hell in the second book, courtesy of a very caring Beast and Walter.

I am afraid there is no quotes for 'little Wren', her nickname by her brother and Gab.

For her creation, Walter had a twin, an alter ego, a female counterpart. Walter and Wendy are very special, this you will learn in the fourth book.

For the trivia, Wendy is the one that flew away with Peter. This is a pure wink to 'Peter Pan'. This is a reference to my childhood influences. Disney all the way before I could grab a book and read. So my Wendy ran away with someone called Peterson.

I haven't told you why I called Paul Peterson that way. Why 'P' is how he is usually referred to?
First, 'P' is irreverent and means what it sounds like. I am not taking the piss revealing this to you.

Cecile.

Cecile is the Au-pair girl of the Workmasters. We only encounter her briefly in the first book of the Saga. The French girl had been living with Caroline Workmaster and her son Michael to help out. The single Caroline is a busy doctor with irregular shifts which rendered an Au-pair girl invaluable.

Cecile is reliable and her nice character is well liked by the entire family. She gets on well with everyone. Her responsibilities range from babysitting to picking up Micky from school, passing by helping him with his homework.

She is mentioned a few times and makes a single appearance. It is when she collects the young Michael after school accompanied by the CIA agent charged to protect them, 'Tango Charlie', that the abduction of the young Archangel happens. While the agent is killed before her eyes, she is beaten up severely for her to let go of the child.

It is a very distressed girl that Azryel questions to know what exactly happened during the abduction, when she arrives at Gab's clinic in an ambulance.

What happened next to that character? She made a full recovery apart for one of her eyes, which lost its sight, and Cecile carried on living with Caroline and Micky until they were asked to move to the tree-house of Gabriel for their own security. She went back to France to see her family before applying for a job in the UK. Cecile lives in Cambridge. We will meet her there, later on in the Saga, for a blessed reunion with the Workmasters and their expending family.

Cecile is not the most important character in the world. She is a background one yet it is nice to have her there, she adds a bucolic concrete reality to the story: from the French nursery songs she teaches to Micky, to her night out once a week as her only demand.

It-666's Saga is embedded in a time frame. The Beast is discovered, age 16, by Walter Workmaster in 2012. This is the start of the Saga. But the Beast's story or history in itself begins even before her birth. Hence the trilogy prequel will allow all readers to know the full picture. As a storyteller, I have the full whack/works in my head. It goes before and beyond. I put my finger and just pointed to a particular heartbeat in the lifeline of It-666's existence. I started her story at a moment which had most resonance to her life: one of her turning points. It is set in the Autumn of 2012.

It is a dark fantasy yet set in a real background, Earth. To give the feel of that, I use some background characters like Cecile, background noises of events or a geographical background. Although I love the later to be most imprecise for the fantasy to infiltrate it with its imaginary magic. My writing is impressionistic rather than realistic down to a T. If I had to compare it with a painting of my favourite painter, J. M. W. Turner, as an example, I would pick 'Rain, Steam and Speed'.

For the trivia in that painting there is a tiny hare running from the steam engine, full of meanings. In the second book, there is a little white rabbit scene running in front of Gab's car, full of meanings too. It's a little winking homage to Turner.

Getting back to Cecile: I was an Au-pair when I arrived in the UK for a couple of years, then a nanny to pay for my university fees. I cherish that time more than I can say. I was made to feel part of my British family so much, that they are family to me. The Au-Pair is a 'clin d'oeil' to my own past.

The character's first name of Cecile is another little wink to my 'souvenirs'. A lot of people called me 'Cecile' not getting my real first name of 'Celine'. I didn't mind the mistake for one bit. I preferred 'Cecile' to 'Celine' for a very personal reason. My parents called me 'Celine' because of a sad song they both loved, the one of Hughes Aufray. When my own life took the shades of sadness similar to the one in the song for years, I yearned to change my name. I did not mind 'Cecile' because it brought a much happier song to memory, 'Cecile, ma fille' of Claude Nougaro. However I chose to become 'Cordelia Malthere', and legalise fully the pen name I was writing under for years. It has much more depth of meaning than a pretty or sad song to me, the one who has to carry it for life.

Let's hear Cecile, a French Au-Pair, like I was, learning English while learning life and looking after children: Blessed time.

The only quote:

'In the emergency room, Gabriel told his staff to leave and closed the door behind Walter Workmaster. Azryel went to the suffering Au-Pair girl, Cecile. He applied a cold compress upon her tumefied cheekbone and asked in French,

-Cecile, ma fille, dis moi ce qu'il s'est passe? Gabriel is a good Doctor. He will tend to your injuries. You will make a full recovery under his hands. Speak, my girl, speak for his nephew is in danger right now.

The girl started crying and pointing to the hospital bed of the killed CIA Agent told,

-They got Tango Charlie. They killed him, the three of them. He had no chance. I was battered until I released Micky from my protection. Meagre, the space of my arms, they broke them. One, a tall bold man, put a chloroform tissue upon little Micky who past away immediately. He took him in a white van with 'Electricity E & E' written upon it. The cropped blonde hair guy gave the final blow to Charlie and jumped into the driver seat of the van. While the Mexican one with a Santa Morte tattoo gave me a blow in the cheek that sent me miles away counting birds in Feather land.

Az asked further,

-As tu entendus leur noms? Their names my dear girl?

The French girl shook her head, replying,

-Code names. No real names. Tattoo guy is known as Scythe. The blonde one was called the Aryan and the bold one was named '3'.

Azryel ordered,

-Gab, stop doing postmortems on Tango Charlie. Cecile is alive and needs your full attention to get well: two broken arms, contusions, a cheek bone fractured, one eye is almost lost and in need of immediate attention.'
(verse 29: Speedy Recovery Company...)

Tango Charlie.

Tango Charlie is a human character which only appears in the first book. CIA/security agent, code name Tango Charlie is one of the Service secret connections of Big Gab and his Uncle Raphael. However if Wrath uses the services of human secret agents with scarcity and sagacity, his nephew prefers using their services to soliciting the ones of the Angels of Raphael. On the part of Gabriel, you may call this pride, or an ongoing feud with Wrath which makes him reluctant to ever have to ask the elder Archangel for help.

So in order to protect Walter Workmaster who by rescuing the Beast put himself and his family in grave danger, Gabriel put all his security agents connections on the case. Of course no words about the existence of It-666 were exchange with the humans agents, Gab used another excuse to enlist their help.

His will to use the humans rather than the Angels, put them into considerable risks and hazards. Tango Charlie's fate is a result of that choice. He dies trying to save Micky from being abducted.

Transported to the clinic of Gabriel, he receives a miraculous intervention: his life is given back to him by the Death Angel who was harangued to do so by an adamant Workmaster who could not accept the death of the man who tried to protect his son. That scene is one of many between Walter Workmaster and Azryel. I relish writing those scenes between the argumentative man and the offstandish, standoffish Angel of Death. The human has a way to get into Az's heart like no other. While the Angel has a way to bring up Walt to his Angelic level, slowly but surely, educating him.

If you will see more interactions between Az and Walt during the entire Saga, as they become strong partners to protect humanity and their loved ones, you will not hear about 'Tango Charlie' anymore.

He is just a minor character. Let's meet him barely mentioned in passages:

'The young It-666 looked piteously at herself but offered a smile and proposed,

-Fight, I can't do much with my human shell right now, Gabriel said it will take three months for me to recover and be able to walk. However I have other ways to fight, which are a bit drastic in a poltergeist sort of way.

Raphael cocking his brows intrigued quizzed her,

-Pray would you mind demonstrating your way of fighting? For the bleeding walls and the flying bed were already quite a tasty appetizer.

Gabriel stood up straight away and intervened,

-No! No demonstration, no main course, especially in my clinic. I know what she can do roughly and let's not try that at home nor anywhere. I will not enjoy a freak show right now, knowing that Micky is in danger and we need to retrieve him fast. I say lets go immediately to P's bunker and break all their necks before they lift a finger to remove Micky's ones.

Azryel Mortimer grinned sarcastically commenting,

-Look whose talking! If it is not the very Archangel who let his very Archangelic little nephew down by giving him the security to be walked to school by a mere man and a young au-pair girl. Did it come to his mind that what men do most easily is dying? No of course not, for Archangel Gabriel likes using mankind in his dealings to keep a little away from being checked thoroughly by his own Angelic kind. It gives him the liberties to keep unusual lab rat like the quote 'Freak' to study and to experiment for himself his discoveries about the freaking powers that do exist, which he would like to possess, by trying them out on his mere human Guinea pigs, with devastating effects. Someone should not be called Archangel, nor Angel but a fallen one and should have his wings cut. For Gabriel, going into P's bunker all guns blazing, is not a good idea. Shall I re-educate you upon being a clever Angelic soldier, one that uses his brain rather than guts instincts? Gosh, I have my work cut out with you. I can't believe how easy it was for you to bow to me my dear Angel. However looking at your soul right now, I know how lost you are and feel.'
(verse 28: About Embracing Death TrUst.)

'Azryel ordered,

-Gab, stop doing postmortem on Tango Charlie. Cecile is alive and need your full attention to get well: two broken arms, contusions, a cheek bone fractured, one eye is almost lost and in need of immediate attention.

Walter who stood by Azryel all along silently, put himself across the door as he saw him about to leave the room, and asked,

-What about Tango Charlie?

Az answered bluntly,

-Flat and dead. It was his time.

Workmaster shook his head negatively,

-It wasn't! He was killed by the will of three men and their Mastermind. Do not tell me that their wills rule fate and the World and that whatever they decide to do will go pass unchecked. Do not tell me that their murderous will is granted as fate and accepted. For all can murder at will and fate does not exist but only free will. Bring that man back to life, give him back his chances, you and I, know that you can. Az, bring Tango Charlie back. He is a good solid man.Please, I beg of you to consider him.

Raphael's benchman smiled ironically and pestered for himself, then out loud,

-Working upon Workmaster is an impossible task. Charlie Tango is a weakest link. His time did come. The man will be dead in any future endeavours. He has no future. Listen if you can, Walter.

Walter shook his head and pointed to the dead CIA agent,

-That man died for the life of my son, I want him alive and well. What about the rewriting of the Scriptures? My re-writing of them? It starts right now. If you can not deflect one man's life course, how are you going to preserve the whole humanity from Evil and the Apocalypse? Are you going to do fate upon us all

and bring Evil to pass as if it was said from high above and set in golden letters that cannot be changed? Or Are you going to use your own free will Angel and re-write it all with Us?

The Death Angel stood by the door shaking his head in a negative fashion before walking to the dead Charlie Tango. He put his hands upon the dead man's chest, recalling him to the living. Cecile's eyes blinked amazed before Gabriel sent her to a level of unconsciousness in which her recent memory would be erased. As he started to tend to her broken arms, he enjoined Azryel with a wicked smile in the angelic tongue,

-Workmaster's way, where will it lead Us? I can take care of those two humans and Walt. Make sure you get to little Micky ASAP. Beware of Bambi. She is a hell of a girl. She seemed tamed but I do not know how tamed she is, or if she really is. But she is the real thing, I have her blood sample in my lab. Get to know a slab before going to get little Micky.

Azryel nodded, pulled Walter out of the room with him and asked,

-Happy? Charlie Tango will make it for another day.

Workmaster queried,

-Just a day? I thought your powers were great. 'Apocalypse Now' it is, then.

Death turned to him and scolded,

-Walter, the man is due. Charlie Tango will not last long whatever I do. There are things your mind will not comprehend. The leeway to work upon them is very slim. I know the leeways but cannot abuse them. I abused one for Charlie Tango for I need to move on to fetch Micky before it is too late. Come, stay behind and look after Caroline, she is very distressed right now, and will be until I bring her son back and alive. I will secure Bambi throughout, do not worry about it. Raphael will make sure all of us, Micky, Bambi and I will come back in one piece. He is coming forward. In Angelic terms, it means he will reveal himself to humans. It also means he is the first warning.

Walter kept the fast stride of the Death Angel and asked worried when he reached It-666 containment room,

-First warning?

Azryel smiled to him sarcastically,

-Not now Workmaster. Long explanation to a human mind, yet alone an Atheist one. I will be there all night and I am needed elsewhere. Long kiss good night, wish me luck, wish that your son has not bled a single drop yet.

Walter grabbed the hand of the Angel and wished,

-With all my heart, go. I just wish what you are wishing. I do not know any better, Az. I will keep an eye on Caroline and provide her the shoulder she needs right now.

The Death Angel disappeared saying to him,

-Good man.'
(verse 29: Speedy Recovery Company...)

Mister '3', 'Santa Morte', the Aryan, henchman Colt and Big Brother 4.

Mister '3', 'Santa Morte', The Aryan, henchman Colt and Big Brother 4 are all humans at the service of Paul Peterson. They are all killers apart for Big Brother 4 who is the security watcher at 'P's'. They are all fearing the demonic politician. They will follow his orders to the letter to save literally their own skins and they will be ruthless about it.

They are the one who abducted little Micky, Workmaster's son, killing Tango Charlie doing so, and beating the crap out of Cecile. They were also the ones, along with 'P' who tortured the Beast for eight years.

Their characters's fates aren't jolly or swinging apart for their falling heads. None makes it past the first two instalments of the Saga.

Santa Morte, full of tattoos of death and The Aryan worshipping by his entire being the Nazi spell, are sent to their deaths swiftly by Azryel's scythe. Mister 3 is the only one left alive, in the big rescue of little Michael. However what he was left to convey, what he saw, renders him, makes him sound like a mad man. 'P' will not leave him that opportunity to spread what he saw, he gets the man's tongue and fingers cut off, rendering his possibility of communicating nil or almost.

Let's not spend a lot of of time talking about small baddies, lets have one passage and move one to the worst of the worst, the mister Big Bad of all time: Eremiel.

'As the henchmen of P were fiercely attacked by dark shadows, Death appeared into the room in his all dark regalia, spreading his black wings. Lifting his scythe he called out,

-Aryan, Santa Morte. You are called upon. Come with me.

A swirl of his scythe made the two heads rolled upon the ground.

The last man standing ran to the door, but could not get it open. When he turned back to face the room all had disappeared but the bleeding walls. The pentagram on the floor was gone. Full of fright and dismay he could not believe his eyes of what just happened. He went to open the trap door to check if It-666 was hiding within. Rats and mice came pouring out of it by the thousands, attacking him. He ran away, managed to get out, and ran very, very far away from the bunker, in shock and breathless.

He will have to report to 'P' the situation and did not look forward to it.' (verse 29: Speedy Recovery Company.)

Eremiel.

Well, here we arrive at a character which I kept in reserve for the last to be mentioned: Eremiel, the father of the Beast, aka, Evil. Fallen Archangel, the extremely handsome Eremiel is bad to an unsettling purity. He is the nasty piece of cake that the Angels have constantly faced for almost an eternity as their Arch-enemy. He ruled Hell for a long while, after being 'fired' by the Tutor and sent there, and after depositing Hades from his Hell throne, shortly afterwards. Eremiel is the evil character in the It-666 Saga: we meet him in all the books written in one form or another. He is that undermining constant Being which wants none to have an 'happy ever after' apart from himself.

Well, he has done enough to never get happiness, so destroying the one of others is the next best thing. He is very good at destroying anything from hope to life. In fact he has become a Master in that matter. Scheming and planning for the destruction of all, gives Eremiel his best orgasm of all time with the demonic goddess Lilith, conceiving the Beast, which is meant to bring the Apocalypse about. Although, the conclusion of it/It all is not going according to his devastating plans.

Thwarting them are mere humans: first, Father Arthur Williamson, who has the guts to curse and abduct his daughter, then much later, Walter Workmaster, who has the guts to adopt the Beast whilst, he is her own father and still alive. To make matters worst, even Angels give a hand to the humans to reinforce their projects to protect humanity. I can not start with a word strong enough which encompasses the boiling anger of Eremiel. For him, his Evil daughter was ruined, spoilt to a non-recognition point, a traitor to destroy, slowly or fast like all others. Worst she is working for Wrath, who he hates with a passion.

The story of Eremiel runs deep into a long history, intertwined with the one of Raphael and Azryel. I will indulged you to a snippet passage of book three, which tells more about it:

'Throwing the leather satchel upon his shoulder, Death pestered,

-Aren't my shoulders very broad? Anything else to be thrown upon them?

Wrath coming by his general tapped his shoulder in a brotherly fashion,

-Yes, make sure they come back to me and fast. Go and stay safe. I will be waiting for you in the yard.

His general grinning to him answered with a wink,

-I will make sure you do not miss overloading them for too long, Raphael.

Jumping upon the back of Armageddon, Death ordered her to spread her wings. Her crimson dragon wings opened straight away, as the Archangelic Beast told,

-She is dying for a good ride!

When his hand tapped the strong neck of the Dra-Rex, Azryel promised before making the creature taking off,

-Is she now? Let's give her one she will remember for I am the Master of good rides, especially the dying great freaking ones. And off we go Babies, see you soon, make sure you will not do anything I would not do.

Seeing the Dra-Rex disappearing in the Hell's sky high ceilings, Asha turned to Wrath with a knowing look and commented,

-The question is what will he not do?

To which the Archangel answered with the most stern and serious look,

-If you knew fully his abilities and what he can do like I do, plenty. Now let's make sure you, Met and Adre get a small rest before dawn. I will stay there with It looking out for Az and any unwelcome intruders like more of Hades's Guards. Give the rest orders and look after this household from the inside. You will have my telepathic call in case of an alert, so be at rest until then, Soldier.

When Asha left the yard, Wrath sat on the bench and enjoined the teenage Beast to do the same as him. She took a place by him, he then added,

-Make yourself comfortable Soldier, nap on my shoulder and let me tell you a bedtime story which might stir you deep down, for it relates to Eremiel, Azryel and I in antediluvian times. Close your eyes, take it in all in, for you are just being given my version of what happened back then. Death behold the version which will not spare any sensibilities. A very long time ago, two Angels were conceived on the same day, one was made out of light, fire and a very specific Angelic essence. This Angel was given many names like a god, as he had within him the divine power to become one. His peers called him Eremiel. As for the second Angel, he was made out of darkness, fire and the very same Angelic Essence. Conceived together, they were meant to be the antipode of each other. When one had flowing blond curls, the other one had raven black ones. When one had the skin the colour of milk, the other one's skin was as black as the night sky. When one's gaze was shimmering like an ocean stroke by noon sun rays, the other was like emeralds set on fire. Both were unusually and strikingly handsome. You will have guessed by now that the second Angel is none but Azryel. Their infancies were miles apart. Death was brought up by a very ancient god in a deep cave, where he was not allowed to see the light of day. From a young age he was trained to answer humanity and creatures' plight. His only companions on his nocturnal outings were wolves. He was taught to sacrifice himself for all Angels and to become the sole beholder of the most dreaded job of all, which was bringing death and dealing with souls. On the other hand, Eremiel was brought up by a goddess who dwelled chiefly in the aether. Petted and encouraged by gods and goddesses to become one of them, Eremiel lived a rather plush existence. While Azryel was a solitary Being, reclusive to the point of shunning the company of others, Eremiel was extremely popular, seeking being the centre of attention and surrounded by followers. Now in the Angelic, Beings and gods society, nothing is a given, you have to earn and deserve everything. The friendless and feared Death Angel was dutiful and hard working. It was not long before he had his own realm. When wars and fights started rampaging the Earth, I was tasked to become another punisher and to bring the wrath of the gods to the sinning human and Beings. This is when I had to learn how to deal with souls and their punishments from Azryel. I would say this is when our working relationship started, and I hated to have to work with him. I found him cold, distant and truly right down intimidating. He would barely talk to me. Yet I also saw the way he cared for the souls he had to take, a deep down kindness, mixed with

sympathy wrapped up by great sadness. On task together, I realised that he would always protect me from the hardest duties, taking them upon himself.

-Why would he do that? Aren't you the strongest being an Archangel?

Looking at the inquisitive eyes, Wrath realised that It was deeply eager to know their Angelic story. He smiled kindly to her as he replied,

-Well, I asked him because I felt demeaned by that attitude. Was I not good enough in his eyes to carry on a task, I thought. If I truly wasn't good then how would I learn to improve by not being allowed to do it. So I challenged him. When I expected him to be arrogant with me and imposing upon me by putting me down, his answer surprised me in a disarming way. He confessed that he did not want to see shadows upon any Angel's smile. I realised then that he was sacrificing his own happiness for the one of all other Angels. If he didn't mix with us for some reason or another yet he deeply cared for us. My irrational hate of him disappeared to be replaced by a profound respect. I could understand why that Angel was given a kingdom, his own Army and so on. Previously I thought it was due to his frightening intelligence which seemed to know everything, but also his extreme powers, and the fact that he was well verse in ancient Magic. However Eremiel possessed all those three attributes but remained without a kingdom. Jealousy driven, the Archangel decided to take for himself whatever he could from Earth itself, destituting humans by the thousands, making them believe he was the God, the one and only, in different places and manners, over several thousands of years. He was set on creating havoc. Prior to that he showed an insane interest in Death's activities, believing that being the son of Darkness did set apart Azryel utterly from the rest. Eremiel started to delve into the darkest magic with the intention of earning a kingdom by it. Having tried to befriend Death in order to learn from him his art, Eremiel's soul fell under the scrutiny of the Ultimate Punisher. Az became extremely worried for the Archangel, so much so that he warned that the Angel was on the verge of falling and that we all needed to catch him back before it happened. Alas, set to follow his own path, refusing all help as offences, Eremiel who could have become a god, was so engrossed in his quest of getting himself a kingdom that he started his crimes. He could not understand why being born on the same day, his success did not match the one of Azryel, him who was the son of Light. Once his jealousy had settled in, it was impossible to make him see things in a different way. In fact, it was his great pride and arrogance, the demeaning way he was treating his followers, Angels and humans

alike, that had put a barrier between him and an earned realm along with a god status.

-I remember the way Eremiel addressed me, during his call that sent me levitating but also when we took him from the Boston sewers, and I did find him extremely unpleasant. My blood is curdling just at the mere thought of it. What he says and how he is saying it is just terrifying, truly devious. There is something I am curious about. It is that Azryel rarely mentioned his realm.

Staring in front of him to no specific point, the Archangel explained,

-The Death Angel gave up everything he had to my custody to prevent any other Angel to fall pray of jealousy and envy. He has access to his realm to deal with the souls there but his castle has been left abandoned since almost the stand off he had with Eremiel. He even entered my service as a slave to make sure none ever uses his titles when addressing him. Staying close to me, he is striving to make sure that no Angel of my Angelic Army ever falls again. He is our Watcher. However to save me from death, and in his subsequent fight, Azryel used extreme powers he should not have condemning himself to be partly damned. He will always remain an Angel but never be raised to an Archangel. Hence this is why I am worried with his will to reuse his ancient magical powers to protect me. For me, he has done enough already for an eternity.

-May I asked what did Azryel do?

-He almost sacrificed his soul in order to assess how far gone was Eremiel, what was the capacity and powers of that Archangel. He nearly put his entire life at risk up until he knew with exactitude the way Eremiel was fighting, pushing him to almost the limit of his resources. When he learnt all he needed, Az stopped the fight by his stunt before it was too late for him. He realised Earth and humanity needed protection but that he could also teach my Angels and I how to do so and train them to defend themselves and eventually tackle Eremiel.

Pouting the Archangelic Beast commented,

-This is not fair that Az was partly damned when his intentions aimed at protecting others.

Wrath ruffling her curls, scolded her kindly,

-My little soldier even Az could tell you that intentions are not everything, the methods you employ to achieve a mean are crucial because you are judged by your actions. The Death Angel of the past did not care as much for his own soul as much as for the souls of all others. That fearsome Being was a loner and very much not liked by almost everyone. Devoid of love and appreciation for his sacrifices and work, Azryel was slowly sliding into a dark despair, he had almost gave up on his own self. After the fight, I took his wounded self to his castle. I was not allowed to fix him up because of what he had done to his Angelic soul. He, himself avoided my eyes with the deepest palpable shame. I was gutted that I could not help there and then the very Angel that rescued me so selflessly. We had our first deep conversation as I laid him on the plank bed without bedding in his so called bedroom. I was astounded by the monastic austerity of the place he took his rest. Asking him where he kept any pillows and covers so I could make him more comfortable, he told me he had none, that he could not rest anyhow because of who he was. He then told me to listen to him attentively. We spoke about the advent of evil Eremiel and Az told me that he will teach all Angels for them to be able to fight, then when this was accomplish to eliminate him, the Grim Reaper before he could complete his damnation that he had used to much dark powers to remain safe. I felt so compelled by his sense of care of all yet that he himself got none, I dared to tell him off for the first time in my eternal life. He received the stern scolding by laughing at my face, and told me where to find the way out in his castle, that he would come to me when he was well enough to teach me and my Army to fight for themselves before he would killed himself as I did not want to dirty my hands by doing the job of removing him. I put an ultimatum to him as I left, that if his intentions were to finish the damnation of his soul by his suicide, he could keep his teaching for himself and take them to his grave. That I would have no desire to see him. However if he wanted his soul to be saved before it was too late for him then I would welcome him with all my heart and help him with all my strength, despite him berating me.

Feeling the sleepy head on his shoulder rolling down to his laps, trying to keep vainly awake, the Archangel stopped talking and stroke the blond curls of It pensively. As her eyes closed, her lips begged,

-Please Master, tell me what did Azryel chose?

Wrath smiled and answered,

-This is an easy one to guess my Child as he trains my Angelic Army since an eternity. Back then the news of the fight had spread like wildfire splitting up Angels severely. Some by fear of Eremiel decided not to oppose him but to join his ranks. The uncertainty in my own Army was great. I was concerned about the ultimatum I gave Death, worried that it would have push him to kill himself sooner rather than to come forward. After all Eremiel dismissed all help before his fall, could it be different for the partly damned Azryel. Would this powerful Angel be humble enough to accept help? Three days after the fight, my despair turned into hope when I saw the barely walking Grim Reaper kneeling by me with a proposal unheard of. He was no Eremiel that could not be stopped onto his tracks. He was not too proud either as he humbled himself more than I ever witnessed before or after. Azryel just surrendered himself to me completely. I have been his Master ever since helping him just as I promised, and he hanged on on his part of soul left like his only treasure and possession worth keeping. He doesn't know it, but he has regained part of his lost soul fighting with this Army. I am keeping this from him however to make him carry on but also to only announced to him the full success when it will occurs.

At the gentle snooze upon his laps Raphael smiled peacefully as he added softly,

-And this is why my little Beast, Azryel who found out about Eremiel more than any other at his own expense is the best Master you can ever wish for.' (book 3, chapter/verse: The Ghouls.)

I hope you enjoyed the story of Wrath, Az and the infamous Eremiel. So the character of Eremiel is not a one off one. He lingers in minds, walls, mirrors, observing his victims, learning about them, readying himself to creep upon them in the most fatal way. Often called the Soothsayer, he has the capacity to invade anyone's mind and talk to it in a pervasive, inducing way. The result, even in the strongest individuals may lead them to become Eremiel's useful object and tool, but also ultimately lead to their death.
He is a user and abuser. As a writer, small details make me create endlessly, like adding colourful threads into a tapestry. I sat in a pub once, well, correction, many times in a pub, but once right by an ex-convict, who had a conversation which was most interesting. The reformed man had a tattoo etched on his forearm: 'What goes

around, comes around.'. A story of karma in itself inked into his own skin. He felt it very deep down: karma. I use the theory of karma throughout my Saga. It affects all the characters, and Eremiel does not escape from it: he is used and abused by his own demons. The irony of it provides some sort of relief to his 'Nastiness'.
P and his Cambion witch Cato have managed the feat to diminish Eremiel, slowly but surely in order to use him as they wish. Yet, they do not have a tame Eremiel for that will never happen. They have a slippery snake on their hands, ready to bite any hands, feeding him or not. With the intervention of Wrath, they lose their precious black mamba. The Archangel retrieves his arch enemy with the little Beast's help to imprison him... The result of that endeavour of Wrath will be disclosed in the later instalments of the It-666's Saga.
Let's end with the final words of Book one:
'As the young woman died below his feet, P offered her precious organ to the snake, which took it all slowly, still pulsating slightly.
He called out in tongue through the darkness of the night, accompanied by the evil pray of his followers,

-It, Dear It-666, Control pan'all to you. Major Hell princess on the loose, your great Father is calling you and forever. Listen, listen, you can only listen to your Father.

Miles away, the sleeping It levitated upon her bed within Purallee's clinic at that very moment. Archangel Raphael stood up straight away, worried,

-What's up now?

It-666 floating within the room woke up. Her demonic black eyes opened upon the room and stared into the darkness as the surrounding walls started bleeding.

Gabriel slapped by his uncle woke up to witness the levitation of It-666 and asked wildly,

-Who did upset the damn girl?

Raphael replied,

-She is doing it by herself. I swear. She was sleeping nicely a minute ago. And

then, she went all levitating. Something is up, Gab. Where is Az when you need him?

Azryel came at that very moment and stood by the door extinguishing his cigar upon the door frame. He watched intently as the levitating girl awoke and started speaking in tongue. He swore,

-Great, we have her Dad on the line. He made a bloody connection to It... Gabriel looked at him very worried, asked,

-How can he? The girl was trashed by him for dead for her past sixteen years.

The Death Angel replied strongly,

-He never trashed her, she was abducted at birth by a fervent priest and nun who aimed to protect the World. He tried to find her via P and he just did. He is talking to her right now. The feat took the death of a fair few humans. It-666 will never be the same again. She has direct contact with Hell from now on. She is going to be a Hell Baby to deal with, of that I am certain... Are we sure about raising the girl up?

The End.'
(verse 37: The Calling: Hell control to It-666.)

The World and Saga of It-666.

You have just met the characters of the first book. You will meet more as the other books get published one after the other. I can tell you already that there is a crowd of characters in the universe of It-666. However you have just been introduced to the principal ones: It-666, Walter Workmaster, Azryel Mortimer, Raphael Wrath and Gabriel Purallee.

I must say that those characters constitute my heart and mind family. All of them bestow individual characteristics of what was my real family. A main member is missing, claimed by death too early, my father. I associate him to my Walter. I will not reveal any more who's who. My real family would have to read the books to find their habits or characteristics good or bad exposed in those characters. Grin: likelihood to happen: I will be dead by then, three of them will never read English. The fourth that can is always god knows where. (Tease: this sounds already like a characteristic of...)

I studied Anthropology at university as well as Archaeological Sciences. I love observing people around me. Working in retail for many years, gave me a mine full of gems, diamonds, just pure real characters to sketch, and write about. Therefore some characters come to me from the streets...

In the same spirit, you will find scattered throughout the Compendiums, my drawings of the characters as I visualise them. Drawing is another way to express myself, which I enjoy. Many caricatures which come from my hand are based on watching the world around me.

Since I wrote the first line of the Saga of 'It-666', many events happened, either personal or worldwide. I draw on those in my writing. May it be a criticism, mention, or drawing a parallel line, the scrupulous might notice those passages. They are my way of digesting the harshness of the present, my own tears dropped in its ocean, my own cry.

Four books of the Saga written, one more in my head ready to be penned, with others in mind, I must say that I feel like on a journey. Hour after hour, writing about It makes my day but also night. Following her downcast footsteps until her chin finally raises to speak her mind, until she faces her first battle, until her young heart manages to spell out that she loves someone big time, etc, has been a sheer enjoyment.

Writing the characters surrounding her, was like creating a magic potion, a come again formula, which will keep me happily awake many nights. I must say the top of the crop, coming with his heady Havana cigars scent, sarcasms by the bucketful, and just his entire attitude, is Azryel, the Death Angel. A scene with him in it will make me see dawn in my garden: Sunrise.

I will not give my top ten of characters here for the Saga. However, Walt, Wrath and Gab are all getting into the list. Walter Workmaster is a joy to write. It's simple humanity, the song of a human heart, a plea, a cry and sometimes a shout. Raphael Wrath is almost the same cry brought louder till one's becomes deaf unless he/she did something about it. If Walt has got only words, Wrath has the power of action. He will use it to change things hopefully for the better. As for Gab, he is not as open and straight forward as Walt and Wrath, he is an underground Angel. He will think outside the box sometimes damaging it big time. I love those three and their interactions.

The World of It-666 is our geographical world with added parallel dimensions and magical physical lands or islands. It is a universe or let's say many from the onset. It is real, complex, magical and exciting.

The first book of It-666 is all about finding her. She presents so many challenges. However she gets adopted by Walter. He makes 'It' alright.

The second book is all about raising her. It is a very cheerful instalment, and was a true pleasure to write. The Beast finds herself being fully taken on board by the tough Angels of Wrath, from army training to participating to their missions. She also finds herself in a true yet very unusual home, the one that welcomes her just the way she is...

The third book is all about It stepping into a massive Hell fight, and how all who embraced her, surround her particular Being with lots of love. Saving that self sacrificing Soldier from Hell becomes a rescue mission: she saved too many by her actions to be given up for dead. Wrath and Azryel will never let that happen until/if It-666 turns bad. To write, I must admit that instalment was exciting but also emotional.

The fourth book is all about...

Just read the Saga and you will know.

Compendiums till the End.

We have reached the end of this first edition of the Compendium. I hope you enjoyed meeting my characters. To resume, they are the ones of my first two published books so far. As the Compendium is far from being fixed and pre-determined, as more of my stories will be released, it will be expanded regularly.

Within the pages of the future editions of the Compendium you will be presented with a world of new characters. From the It-666 Saga, Book 2, 'Raising It-666: the Teenage Beast.', soon to be published (August 2015) we have an array of new comers to meet from Cato the Witch and her Army of monsters, the Swallowers, to Metatron, the 'Legolas' looking like Angel, a fan of Tolkien, who drives The Angels of Wrath to their missions in his tweaked super-van, passing by California dwelling Goddess Demeter, a formidable White Witch, surrounded by her devoted servants, a house full of virginal maids.

From book 3, 'Saving It-666: The Archangelic Beast', which will be released in December 2015, the discovery of characters continues. Demon Zeus is introduced with fracas as he brings terror, destruction and chaos in his path. This is an instalment which also sees the resurrection of a demonic creation to life by the Beast, her formidable Dra-Rex, the half dragon-half T-rex monster that she pets like a common dog...

So yes as the journey continues for It-666 from book to book, but also as it carries on in whimsical cursed Wilton Town, the Compendium of Characters will grow and grow and grow... Fans will be able to find the latest version on my website, www.cordelia-malthere.co.uk, as it evolves and before being published; free for all to be enjoyed at any time.

First because it is not only the Beast Saga and the one of Wilton Town that lives in my mind. There are others, some partly written, like the dark fantasy 'Clementine Boatswain's epic adventures in the After-World', and a few more novels and trilogies, some are there waiting for their time to be written up...

Imagine you are on a probing space craft. It lands on a very organic and pulsating planet shaped like two brains sown together. Yep, that's an analogy a tad gruesome, I must admit. But yet the planet has a pretty pink colour marbled by blue and purple veins. From its surface, you see more universes than you ever thought existed with great awe. 'Ground Control' sent you the order to dig deeper. Your craft goes into the unknown, diving into one of the longitudinal fissure of the new planet. No need to drill those brainy grounds, it has the ready inviting shaft, fully formed, leading you to countless side galleries and corridors, a labyrinth of them... You will not know where to start but for the fully illuminated tunnels exposed to your exploration. That living planet is called 'My Mind', the probing craft the 'Compendium'. It will land again and again to explore the new galleries full of gems and light.

Second because it is all about an ever growing imagination creating new worlds and their inhabitants. However if we spoke mainly of the characters in this Compendium, the future ones will have sections dedicated to their geographical worlds but also stories.

Third and last, the Compendium is very much a book which will evolve through time. Only at my death, you will have the definite set edition in your hands as I leave the world. But it will not happen any time soon, I hope, for I have so much writing work to deliver to the big wide world.

From my own experiences I know life can be so short, that fear of acting upon your dreams or goals is not an option. Within a space of three years, I lost three very important people in my life, one being my dad, two being snatched away by cancer. My father was 62, from a generation of arc welders building oil rigs like 'Petrobras', submarines like 'the Pearl', who had a layer of asbestos in their protecting masks, breathing their death sentences as they built for years. Nothing could be done, just watch the man disappear slowly. His grave faces the sea port, he worked and loved, giving a view of the Channel and coastline, he cherished. I am publishing this 'Compendium' on the sad second anniversary of his death, an homage to my father, to commemorate his sad passing, the one who made me. To my Dad, I will live to the full, and write until the end.

To you all, live and love to the full: Make sure you enjoy your journey doing so. Make sure you look back proudly able to say, I contributed to a loving humanity.
Just love that's what it is all about. Love: a four letter word that means life, against its antithesis, hate which means death to all humanity.

To that I will finish with:
Lots of love to you all,
See you soon at my next Compendium.
Thank you for reading my works,
From the bottom of my heart,
Lots of kisses,
Xxxx

Cordelia Malthere.

By the same author:

Finding It-666: The Beast

Book One of the teenage Antichrist years.

Born on the 06/06/1996 in London, the young It is a sweet sixteen supernatural Being of a special kind, one meant to bring the end of the human world: the Beast incarnated, the Antichrist.

Fall 2012, the Beast was found. From the deep darkness of her hole, she is raised up to the light. From her closed cage below a pentagram made of blood, she is freed. The human who found her, Walter Workmaster, is a firm atheist, a private investigator and former human rights lawyer who becomes her staunch advocate. Adopting the lost It, the man released her to his world to make her face humanity and unknowingly much more... The advent of the Beast has started. Step one, she is found.

Hair Rising, Heir Raising, Erasing.

By Cordelia Malthere.

A vibrant beyond the grave tale which will chill your bones while warming your heart. When the deadly serious is delightfully hilarious, you will know you have just been acquainted with Abraham Wilton-Cough. His skeletal hand will drag you from grave to grave, under the moonlight of the night where many dead are rising... Could it be the apocalypse?

Coming Soon:

Raising It-666: The teenage Beast

Book Two of the young Beast years.

Adopted by the human Walter Workmaster, the Beast is being given a fair chance to live and learn almost like a normal teenager. 'Almost', for normality does not apply when It-666 is concerned. Trained to be a Soldier by the Angel of Death, monitored by Archangel Raphael and looked after by Archangel Gabriel, It is raised as a Being with the open opportunity of her own heart, which they will protect. Trips to Hell and fighting demons make her earn her true colours within the Angelic Army raising her up in their midst.

Printed in Great Britain
by Amazon